Book 2 in the Once Upon a Dickens Christmas series

A TALE *of* TWO HEARTS

MICHELLE GRIEP

SHILOH RUN PRESS
An Imprint of Barbour Publishing, Inc.

Print ISBN 978-1-68322-259-0

eBook Editions:
Adobe Digital Edition (.epub) 978-1-68322-912-4
Kindle and MobiPocket Edition (.prc) 978-1-68322-913-1

Cover Design: Kirk DouPonce, DogEared Design

Published by Shiloh Run Press, an imprint of Barbour Publishing, Inc., 1810 Barbour Drive, Uhrichsville, Ohio 44683, www.shilohrunpress.com

Our mission is to inspire the world with the life-changing message of the Bible.

Member of the
Evangelical Christian
Publishers Association

Printed in Canada.

PRAISE FOR
A TALE OF TWO HEARTS

A lovely tale of second chances, surprises, and love that will leave you with a sweet sigh of satisfaction. Perfect for Dickens fans at Christmas or any time of year.

—Julie Klassen, bestselling author

Michelle has an incredible knack of being able to twist mystery, romance, and historical detail into a giant ball of extraordinary fun! Not to be missed by fans of Dickens. Or anyone else for that matter!

—MaryLu Tyndall, bestselling author of
the Legacy of the King's Pirates series

A Tale of Two Hearts invites your heart to go on a wild roller-coaster ride. Trapped in a lie, can they find their way out before irreparable damage is done? Add to the plot sweet Uncle Barlow, adorable Miss Whymsy, and a pair of deplorable cousins, and you've got a story your heart won't forget.

—Ane Mulligan, award-winning author of the Chapel Springs series

A Dickensian delight! Victorian London and the characters within come alive within these pages. I thoroughly enjoyed riding the characters coat-tails through bustling streets between the Golden Egg Inn, Purcell's Tea Room, and more as they wove a tangled web of their own design—and then desperately tried to unravel it before falling through the strands. A refreshing tale perfectly paired with a cup of Christmas tea.

—Jocelyn Green, award-winning author of *A Refuge Assured*

When a seemingly harmless deception escalates to alarming proportions, the characters in *A Tale of Two Hearts* are forced to question their values and decide if sacrificing their integrity justifies the altruistic outcome. This delightful story combines a host of interesting characters, fresh writing, and a heartwarming ending that will leave the reader smiling.

—Susan Anne Mason, award-winning author of
Irish Meadows and *A Most Noble Heir*

In *A Tale of Two Hearts*, Michelle Griep tells a skillfully woven tale both elegant and heartwarming. Charles Dickens would be delighted with the way she tucked into this story's pockets truths and observations he penned long ago. Highly recommended reading, no matter the season.

—Cynthia Ruchti, author of *An Endless Christmas*, *Restoring Christmas*, and more than twenty other novels and nonfiction

Delightful Christmas fare perfect for fans of English historicals, brimful with Dickensian details and the beautiful Christian truth of second chances.

—Carolyn Miller, author of Regency Brides: Legacy of Grace and Regency Brides: A Promise of Hope series

I have found another favorite author and it's Michelle Griep. With an incredible ability to spin a beautiful tale, Griep sucked me into the story from the very first paragraph. From the historical detail to the English setting to the unforgettable and enjoyable characters, I didn't want to put this book down. William and Mina will stick with me for a long time. This will be a story to read again and again. And now I'm off to find every Michelle Griep book I can get my hands on.

—Kimberley Woodhouse, bestselling author

Just when you think you're about to embark on a cheeky, fun Christmas lark, you realize what a multifaceted, complex story Griep has crafted. With characterizations Dickens would envy, and bright, fresh writing that pulls you in, *A Tale of Two Hearts* will have you cheering on Mina and William and appreciating the skill with which they have been wrought.

—Erica Vetsch, author of *A Perfect Christmas* in *The Victorian Christmas Brides Collection*

A heartwarming tale of second chances coming from the least expected places. I loved the many nods to Dickens and the inventive twists on a few other classics. In *A Tale of Two Hearts*, romance isn't only for the young, and fresh starts aren't only for the faultless. An uplifting and charming holiday story!

—Jennifer Delamere, author of *The Captain's Daughter*

CHAPTER ONE

London, 1853

Whether I shall turn out to be the hero of my own life,
or whether that station will be held by anybody else,
these pages must show.
David Copperfield

I n the tiny back courtyard of the Golden Egg Inn, Mina Scott
lowered her copy of *David Copperfield* to her lap and lifted her
face to the October sun. Closing her eyes, she savored the warmth
and the first line to a new adventure, as was her wont whenever
Miss Whymsy stopped by and lent her a book. Though she no
longer stared at the page, the shapes of the words lingered, blazed
in stark contrast to the brilliance against her lids. What a curious
thought, to be one's own hero—for the only hero she wanted was
William Barlow.

Ahh, William. Just thinking his name lit a fire in her belly.

"Mina!"

She shot to her feet, and the book plummeted to the ground.
Her stomach dropped along with it—both for being caught idle
and for the dirt smudges sure to mar the cover. With her toe, she
slid the novel beneath her skirt hem, then patted her pocket to
make sure the note Miss Whymsy had left behind hadn't fallen out
as well. The small, folded paper crinkled beneath her touch, hidden
and snug. Satisfied, she faced her father.

Jasper Scott, master of the inn and commander of her life, fisted
hands the size of kidney pies at his hips. "What are ye doin' out in

the yard, girl, when ye ought to be serving?"

She dipped her chin. "It's hardly teatime, Father. I thought to take a break before customers arrived." From the peak of the inn's rooftop, a swallow not yet flown to warmer climates chided the frail excuse. Not that she blamed the bird. It was a pitiful defense.

Her father fumbled his big fingers inside a small pocket on his waistcoat and pulled out a worn brass pocket watch. He flipped open the lid—and the whole thing fell to the ground. "Oh, bother!"

As he bent to pick it up, she stifled a smile. How large Father's grin would be on Christmas Eve when he opened the new watch fob she'd been saving all her pennies for.

Swiping up the dropped watch, Father first frowned at the time, then at her. "It's past tea." He snapped the timepiece shut and tucked it away. "I wager ye were reading again. Am I right?"

How did he know? How did he *always* know?

Slowly, she retrieved the book and held it out. "Maybe you ought to keep this until we close tonight."

"I thought as much when Miss Whymsy stopped by. Keep your head in the world, girl, not in the clouds. Ye'll never get a husband that way." He snatched the novel from her hand. "And besides that, this being the last day o' October, ye must turn yer sights away from make-believe tales and toward Christmas. Only a little over seven weeks remain to make this the best celebration the Golden Egg has ever seen, so ye must focus, girl. Now off with ye. There are patrons already clamoring for a whistle wetting."

"Yes, Father." She scurried past him. Since she'd been a little girl, the annual Christmas Eve celebration at the Golden Egg meant everything to Father. 'Twas a poor replacement for her departed mother, but a replacement, she supposed, nonetheless. She darted through the back door and nearly crashed into Martha, the inn's cook.

"Peas and porridge!" Martha stepped aside, the water in her pot sloshing over the rim and dampening the flagstones. "Watch yer step, missy."

"Sorry, Martha." Giving the woman a wider berth, she grabbed her apron from a peg and a cloth for wiping tables, then scooted out to the taproom.

Once she entered the public area, she slowed her steps and drew a deep breath. No one liked to be waited upon by a ruddy-cheeked snippet of a skirt. Scanning the room, she frowned. Only two tables were filled. Surely Father could've managed to wait upon these few—

Her gaze landed on her brown-haired hero, and her heartbeat increased to a wild pace. William Barlow leaned forward in a chair, deep in conversation with the fellow seated adjacent to him—his friend, Mr. Fitzroy. Will's presence lit the dull taproom into a brilliant summer landscape simply by merit of his presence—especially when he threw his head back and laughed. And oh, what a laugh. Carefree and merry, as if he'd reached out his hand and pulled her into a jig with the lightness of it.

Mina grabbed a pitcher and filled it with ale, the draw of William too strong to deny. Bypassing the other customers, she headed straight for his table.

"He's invited me to a tea, of all things." His voice, smooth as fresh flowing honey, grew louder the closer she drew to his table. "Can you imagine that, Fitz? A tea. How awful."

A smile curved her mouth as she imagined taking tea with William. Just the two of them. Him in his finest frock coat with a snowy cravat. Her in a new gown. She'd pour a steaming cup for him, and he'd lift a choice little cake to her lips while speaking of his deepest affections. She sighed, warm and contented. "I should think a tea would be very pleasant," she murmured.

Both men turned toward her. Mr. Fitzroy spoke first. "Well, if it isn't the lovely Miss Scott, come to save me from this boorish fellow." He elbowed William.

Will arched a brow at her, a rogue grin deepening the dimples at the sides of his mouth. "I was wondering when you'd grace us with your appearance, sweet Mina."

Sweet Mina. Heat flooded her cheeks. She'd be remembering that endearment in her dreams tonight.

But for now, she scowled. "Mr. Barlow, if my father hears of your familiarity, I fear—"

"Never fear." He winked—and her knees weakened. "I'm a champion with ruffled fathers."

Ignoring his wordplay, she held up the pitcher. "Refills?"

William slapped his hand to his heart. "You know me too well."

Not as well as I'd like to. She bit her tongue. Where had that come from? Maybe Father was right. Maybe she had been reading too many books.

"I'm as intrigued as Miss Scott." Mr. Fitzroy held his cup out to her, for she'd filled William's mug first. "Why would you not want to attend your uncle's tea? As I recall, he's a jolly enough fellow."

Will slugged back a long draw of his ale and lowered his cup to the table. "Nothing against Uncle Barlow, mind you. And in truth, I was pleased he'd made contact. It's just that, well. . .I am to bring my wife along."

Wife!

The pitcher clattered to the floor. Mina stared at it, horrified. Ale seeped into the cracks of the floorboards, the very image of her draining hopes and dreams. William Barlow had a wife?

Will shot to his feet. "Mina, you look as if you've seen the Cock Lane ghost. Are you ill?"

"I'm f–fine. The pitcher—it slipped, that's all." She crouched, righted the pitcher to preserve the remaining ale, then yanked the rag from her waistband and mopped up the mess with more force than necessary. The scoundrel! All this time he'd had a hearth and home already tended by a wife? Did he have children as well? She scrubbed harder, grazing her knuckles against the rough wood.

Good. She relished the pain and for a wicked moment thought about swishing the spilled ale over William's shoes.

"Wife?" Surprise deepened Mr. Fitzroy's voice also. So. . .Will's best friend had not known either? That was a small satisfaction, at least.

"This is news," Mr. Fitzroy continued. "When did that happen?"

Holding her breath, she ceased her scrubbing, though why she cared indicted her for being naught but a dunderheaded hero seeker. *Silly girl. Silly, stupid girl.*

William sank back to his seat. "Well, I don't actually have one yet. And that's the problem."

"Thank God." The words flew out before she could stop them, and she pressed her lips tight.

William's face appeared below the table. "Are you quite all right?"

"Yes. Just finishing up." She forced a smile, reached for the runaway pitcher, and stood. This afternoon was turning into a novel in its own right. For the first time since she'd met William, she couldn't decide if he were truly a hero or a villain.

Will straightened as well, his gaze trained on her. The sun slanted through the front window, angling over his strong jaw and narrow nose. But it was his eyes that drew her. So brilliant, so magnificently blue, a sob welled in her throat. She swallowed. She truly was a silly girl.

"Say, Mina," he drawled. "You wouldn't be willing to be my bride, would you?"

"I—I—" The words caught in her throat like a fish bone, and she coughed, then coughed some more. Heat blazed through her from head to toe. Surely, she hadn't heard right.

William's grin grew, his dimples deepening to a rakish angle. "Oh, don't panic. It would only be for one afternoon. Surely you could beg off serving for an hour a week from next Thursday?"

Her mouth dropped, but no words came out. What was she

to say to that? Everything in her screamed to shout yes, but how could she possibly slip out from beneath Father's notice? And a week from next Thursday? Not that her social calendar was packed full, but something niggled her about the date.

"Oy, miss! Another round over here." Across the taproom, a stout fellow, buttons about to pop off his waistcoat, held a mug over his head.

"I—I don't know," she blurted out to Will and turned.

But William grasped her sleeve. "Please, Mina. Allow me to explain. It won't take but a moment."

She stared at his touch, a frown tugging her lips. Father wouldn't like her dawdling with William, but how could she refuse the man she'd cast as the champion in every story she'd read? With a quick nod and a brilliant smile to stave off the other customer, she turned back to Will. "Make haste. I have work to attend."

"Right, here's the thing." He leaned forward, the excitement in his tone pulling both her and Mr. Fitzroy closer to him so that they huddled 'round the table.

"Uncle Barlow is ready to choose his heir. It's between me and my cousin Percy—"

"Egad!" Mr. Fitzroy rocked back on his chair. "That pompous donkey? I should think there'd be no competition."

"I agree, but my uncle favors a married man. And since I am not..." Will tugged at his collar, loosening his cravat. "Well, I gave Uncle Barlow the impression I'd recently wed, or I'd not even be considered."

Mr. Fitzroy let out a long, low whistle.

Mina's eyes widened. "You lied to your uncle?"

William shook his head, the tips of his hair brushing against his shoulders. "No, not outright. I merely led him on a merry word chase, and he arrived at a particular conclusion."

Mr. Fitzroy chuckled. "One day, my friend, your deceptions will catch up to you."

"Perhaps. But not today. Not if you, my sweet Mina"—William captured her free hand and squeezed—"will agree to be my wife for the tea. I could pick you up at two o'clock. What do you say?"

Say? How could she even think with the warmth of his fingers wrapped around hers and his blue gaze entreating her to yield? It would be lovely to live a fairy-tale life if only for part of an afternoon. Take tea in a grand house, finally be a real lady, just like those she so often read about—

"Miss!" the man across the room bellowed again.

—*And* escape the drudgery of serving corpulent patrons who more often than not smelled of goats and sausages.

Pulling her hand away, she smiled at William. "I say yes."

God bless her! For surely her father wouldn't. Before Will could say anything more, she scurried off to fill the other patrons' mugs and drain her pitcher dry. On her way back to the tap, she swerved around a table, and her gown brushed against her hand. Paper crinkled at the contact.

Then she knew.

Setting the pitcher down on the counter, she glanced over her shoulder to make sure no one was looking before she retrieved the note from her pocket. A moan caught in her throat as she reread the instructions:

Sisterhood meeting November 10th
2:00 p.m.

Drat! That was a week from next Thursday. How was she to be in two places at once?

CHAPTER TWO

I have been bent and broken, but—I hope—into a better shape.
Great Expectations

No matter the time of day, London streets teemed as if a great bucket of humanity had been upended and dumped onto the sidewalks. And late afternoon was the worst. Cabs, drays, and coaches filled the cobblestones, forcing pedestrians to travel as far from the gutters as possible, lest they be splashed with liquid refuse of all sorts. William Barlow not only took it all in stride but relished the challenge as well. A good leg stretcher, that's what he needed—especially after the ridiculous proposal he'd just issued to Mina Scott. What in the queen's name had he been thinking?

"Hold up!" Fitz's voice turned Will around—his sudden stop earning him a scowl and a curse from a fishy-smelling sailor who smacked against him.

The man gave him a shove as he passed. "Watch yer step, ye carpin' swell."

Ten paces back, Fitz dodged a knife-seller's cart, one hand holding his hat tight atop his head, and caught up to Will. "I didn't realize this was a race."

"Sorry. My mind was elsewhere."

"Hmm, let me guess. Somewhere back at an inn with a certain blue-eyed beauty?"

Will clouted his friend on the back, and they fell into step together. "You can't be serious. Mina Scott is a sweet girl. Nothing more."

"As I suspected. And now that Miss Scott is out of ear range, how about you tell me the real reason for such a scheme?"

Will shrugged. "I don't know what you're talking about."

"Don't play the innocent with me. Ever since Elizabeth, you've avoided anything to do with women other than lighthearted banter, and you've never given Mina Scott a second thought. Something else is going on here, something mighty powerful to be prodding you to play the part of a husband."

Thankfully, they stepped off a curb to cross Bramwell Street, where it took all of William's concentration to weave in and out of traffic unscathed. And just as well—for he'd rather not dwell in the unforgiving land of memories.

Once across, Fitz joined his side, with only somewhat muddy trouser hems to show for the experience. "You know I won't be put off so easily."

That was an understatement. When Thomas Fitzroy was set on something, there was no turning the man back—a trait that served his friend well down at Temple Court. Even so, Will plowed through a few more pedestrians before he answered. "I told you everything. Uncle Barlow is—"

"Yes, yes." Fitz waved his fingers in the air like an orator making a point. "Uncle Barlow, what have you, and so on and so on. Not that I don't believe every word you said, but I suspect there are a few more words you've conveniently left out. So let's have it."

He snorted. "Perhaps you should have been a barrister instead of a law clerk."

"Perhaps you should get to the point."

Jamming his hands into his coat pockets, Will stared straight ahead. Better that than witness the pity that was sure to fill his friend's eyes once he told him. "It's my mother. She's not doing well. I can barely keep abreast with her medical bills, let alone continue to manage her housing expenses."

"Oh. . ." Fitz's feet shuffled. "Sorry, old chap. I didn't realize. Is she that bad off?"

"Hard to say. You know doctors." He shook his head as the last of October's light faded into the first gloam of evening. "I shall have to move her from France, which will mean setting up a household of my own instead of rooming with you." He sighed. "And that will come with a hefty price tag."

"I see. No wonder this whole inheritance thing is so important to you."

"It is. Don't get me wrong. I don't wish any ill on Uncle Barlow. Quite the contrary. I hope the old fellow lives a great many more years. But were I to be named heir, I'd have the collateral of the position if I must apply to a banker for funds. Lord knows I wouldn't get a penny on my name alone."

His friend's hand rested on Will's shoulder, slowing him to a stop. Will braced himself for the concern sure to be etched on Fitz's brow. But despite his preparation, he sucked in a breath at the sympathy welling in the man's eyes.

"I hope for your sake, and your mother's, that this all works out."

"Indeed." He cleared the huskiness from his voice and forced a half smile. "Let us hope so."

"But I feel I'd be remiss if I didn't mention this." Fitz rubbed the back of his neck. "Miss Scott is a beauty, no doubt. And ladylike. She's been nothing but kind and ever attentive. Yet is she the right sort of woman to impress your uncle as a realistic bride? She is an innkeeper's daughter, after all. Not exactly a highborn miss. And she's nothing like. . . Well, you know."

While it was a champion thing of his friend to voice his misgivings so earnestly, Will cast Fitz's cares aside. Mina Scott would charm Uncle Barlow, perfect manners or not, for she was a perfectly charming sort of girl.

"Maybe so, Fitz, but you have to admit she is a genteel sort of woman, well spoken and well read. And besides"—he shrugged—"there's no one else to ask."

The truth of his words hit home. Pulling away, he strode ahead.

There *was* no one else to ask, and if this didn't work, how would he ever pay for his mother's increasing care? Even with Mina Scott's help, it would take a miracle for him to be named heir. He'd not even seen his uncle in over a year—a relationship he'd like to mend but didn't quite know how for the shame that still haunted him.

Last time he'd seen Uncle Barlow was when the man had bailed him out of gaol.

CHAPTER THREE

If there be aught that I can do to help or aid you, name it,
and on the faith of a man who can be secret and
trusty, I will stand by you to the death.
Master Humphrey's Clock

It was a grisly kind of day. The type of gloomy afternoon that stuck in one's craw and worked one's teeth to keep the cold at bay. Autumn was such a fickle friend: warm one day, frigid the next. Today, November's rude manners chased away the remnants of October's warmth. Mina tugged her collar tight against her neck as she dashed down the street.

Two blocks from the Golden Egg, she clutched her skirts in one hand and trotted up the stairs to a grey-stone lodging house. As soon as she ducked inside the entrance hall, she removed her veil and shrugged out of her black cape, hanging both on a peg near the door. The other ladies should already be here and wouldn't notice her dark wraps, or she'd have to field a surplus of questions, the chief one being, Who died? Her mourning cloak and veil would be a good disguise on the street when she later waited for William, but here?

Not at all.

She hurried up the stairs, passed the first floor, and stopped on the second. Halfway down the corridor on the left, she paused in front of a door with chipped paint and rapped thrice—twice—once. The door swung open, and she entered the meeting room of the Single Women's Society of Social Reform—which looked an awful lot like a bedchamber. The occupant, her friend Miss Whymsy, greeted her with a smile. The former governess was a plain-faced woman with steel-grey hair and posture that would make a marine look like a slouch.

"Welcome, my dear." Miss Whymsy pulled her into a prim embrace, smelling of lavender and well-used books. "We were beginning to think you might not make it."

"My deepest apologies." She pulled away with a sheepish smile, for it had been her request that the meeting be moved to an hour earlier than first announced. "Father kept me later than I expected, and it was hard to beg off without rousing his suspicions."

"No apology needed. I am glad you are here no matter the time." Miss Whymsy swept out her hand. "Please, have a seat."

Mina crossed the small room to an even smaller sitting area. Three other ladies perched on chairs near the tiny hearth, soaking in what warmth could be had from the sparse bit of burning coal and from the teacups clutched in their hands. Mina took an empty chair next to Effie Gedge, one of her dearest friends. Her skirt hardly touched the seat before Effie leaned toward her and whispered, "I so hate to see another one go."

"Me too." Mina's gaze landed on the woman across from her, and she couldn't help but wonder how Mary Bowman was holding up, this being her last meeting. Apparently, not too well, for after naught but a flickering smile, Mary stared into her teacup, as if all the courage in the world might be found there.

Miss Whymsy settled on the last remaining chair and lifted her chin. "I call this meeting to order, ladies."

Next to Effie, Miss Minton, every bit as grey-haired as Miss Whymsy, chortled a "Hear, hear," and set her teacup on the floor beneath her chair.

"Now then," Miss Whymsy continued, "as you all know, today's gathering is bittersweet. While we are happy one of our members is soon to be off on a journey of matrimonial bliss, it is always a bit of a sorrow to see one of our colleagues leave. Yet it is necessary if we are to remain the *Single* Women's Society of Social Reform."

"Hear, hear," Miss Minton rattled off again.

Miss Whymsy lifted a brow at her before she shifted her gaze to Mary. "Miss Bowman, you have served the society well these past years, and we thank you for your service."

"Yes, thank you," Mina and Effie said together.

"Hear, hear—"

"Millie." Miss Whymsy skewered Miss Minton with a stare that could knock the fidget out of a child. "You do not have to 'hear, hear' everything I say."

"If it is good enough for Parliament"—Miss Minton bunched her nose, adding wrinkle upon wrinkle to her face—"I should think it is good enough for us."

Miss Whymsy blew out a sigh, and Mina stifled a smile. The two were a cat and dog pair, always scuffling and ruffling, yet, at the end of the day, more often than not were willing to share a saucer of milk together.

"Pressing on." Miss Whymsy cleared her throat. "Miss Bowman, have you any parting words?"

Mary stood, though she was hardly taller than her chair even when she arose. Mina's heart squeezed. She would love to be married—especially to Will—yet when that day came, *if* it came, she would miss this fellowship, and judging by the trembling bottom lip on Mary, she would miss them too.

Bravely, Mary smiled at each of them in turn. "Ladies, it has been my joy to serve with you, and I thank you for the opportunity. I shall never forget any of you, my sisters, and though I will be married"—a lovely flush of pink flamed on her cheeks—"I shall endeavor to always look for ways to help downtrodden women everywhere."

"Well said." Mina smiled.

"I'll miss ye." Effie sniffed.

"Hear, hear." This time Miss Minton challenged Miss Whymsy with an arched brow.

Miss Whymsy ignored it. "Godspeed, Miss Bowman. You go with our blessings."

They all stood, and each one hugged Mary before she exited the room. Mina's gaze lingered on the door long after it closed, conflicting emotions roiling in her stomach. It would be lovely to walk out of here into the arms of a husband. Yet the bonds she'd made with these women would leave a mark once broken.

"Our next, and last, order of business for today is a new project." Miss Whymsy rushed ahead before Miss Minton could utter another *hear, hear*. "I have been approached by the director of the Institute for the Care of Sick Gentlewomen."

Effie's teacup rattled on her lap. "But how would a gent know of us? I thought the whole point o' our society was to remain secret, doing deeds unannounced, just like the good Samaritan."

"Don't worry, Miss Gedge." Miss Whymsy leaned across and patted Effie's knee. "I have taken care to keep all of your identities secret, referring to you simply by the first letter of your last name. You are Miss G, Mina is Miss S, and of course Miss Minton is Miss M."

Mina eyed Miss Whymsy over the rim of her teacup. "Pardon me, but isn't that slightly confusing?"

"Not at all. I can keep you straight, and I don't think it will matter to the director"—her gaze drifted to Effie—"who happens to be a woman, not a gentleman."

Effie gasped. "A lady?"

"Indeed."

Mina's cup tinkled against the saucer as she set it down, the glorious possibility of such a position sending a charge through her. Perhaps life could be more than serving mugs of ale at an inn—for clearly this woman, whoever she was, had found a way to do something important with her life.

"What is it the director would like us to do?" she asked.

"That's just it. I don't think we can possibly manage to do all she asks. The institute is growing at such an alarming rate that they are short on staff, funding, and housing. I am happy to volunteer my services, for the hospital mainly cares for my own kindred—retired governesses—and I suspect, Miss Minton, that you would be perfect for that role as well. Rolling bandages or serving tea and the like."

A smile spread broad and bright on Miss Minton's face. "Hear! Hear!"

This time, Miss Whymsy smiled as well. "Good. That takes care of the volunteering. Mina and Effie, is there any way the two of you would be able to help out?"

"Well," Effie tapped her teacup with her finger, clearly deep in thought, then stopped abruptly. "I've got it! As ye know, being that I'm a lady's maid, I have a fair amount o' castoffs from my employer. I could see my way to parting with a few. Talk is, Bagley's Brokerage in the Houndsditch Market is the place to sell. I'm sure I can wheedle a fair penny for some gowns."

Miss Whymsy clapped her hands. "Brilliant thinking, Miss Gedge." Her gaze drifted to Mina. "Have you any thoughts on the matter? I realize this may be a bit forward, but I feel I must at least bring it up. . . . Is there any chance of housing some of the women at your father's inn?"

She shook her head before Miss Whymsy could finish, a rudeness on her part, yet entirely unstoppable. Father would never allow such an unprofitable use of space, especially before Christmas. "I don't think that's a possibility."

"I see. . . ." Miss Whymsy's voice tapered to nothing.

The ensuing silence poked her conscience like little needles. The two older ladies would be volunteering their time. Effie could donate money. And she'd offered nothing but a big fat no. Yet what could she do? Oh, that she were a wealthy woman, able to bless others out of a storehouse of coins.

She bit her lip, picturing her tiny crock at home filled with shillings and pence—all the money she'd saved these past three years to purchase a new fob for Father's watch. . .a fob her mother had dearly wanted to purchase before her death. Since a girl, it had been Mina's dream to make her mother's wish come true. Should she sacrifice it for the sake of a request by a director she didn't even know?

But as she looked from Miss Whymsy's expectant face to Miss Minton's, the wrinkles carved into their parchment skin were a stark reminder that other women—*sick* women—were in need of that money. More than Father needed a fob, for had he not lived this long without one?

She sighed and, before she could change her mind, said, "I have a small amount on hand at home that I could contribute."

"Wonderful!" Miss Whymsy beamed. "That covers staffing and funding. And as for the housing, well, let's pray about it, shall we?"

Bowing their heads, they set the needs of the institute before the Lord, primarily the housing concern, then went on to bless Miss Bowman's upcoming marriage.

Miss Whymsy ended with an "Amen," and Miss Minton with a rousing "Hear, hear!"

"I believe that officially concludes this meeting. Ladies?" Miss Whymsy stood and held out her hand.

Each of them rose, forming a small circle, and put one of their hands atop the others' in the center. In unison, they lifted their voices. "To God's glory and mankind's good, use our hands and feet in service, oh Lord. Amen."

Before anyone could speak further, Mina edged toward the door. "As much as I'd love to stay and visit, I have to run. Do forgive me. Good afternoon, ladies."

"But Mina—"

She shut the door on Effie's voice, wincing at her own

impropriety. But it couldn't be helped. If she didn't dash out of here now, she'd never make it on time to meet William Barlow's carriage.

But even if she were to run, she'd still be late, for the bong of the downstairs clock chimed two.

CHAPTER FOUR

Oh Sairey, Sairey, little do we know wot lays afore us!
Martin Chuzzlewit

Mina huddled closer to a streetlamp. The cold, iron pole offered little protection against the afternoon's bluster, but her black veil and cape might blend in with the dark pillar so she'd not draw undue attention. Hopefully.

Where was William? She hadn't been that late getting to the corner—only five minutes. Surely he would have waited that long.

Fighting the urge to lift her veil and survey the lane, she forced herself to remain statuesque—especially when pedestrians strode past. She'd taken the precaution of instructing Will to meet her five lanes away from the Golden Egg, but still. . . If one of her friends— or worse, Father's friends—chanced by and recognized her, she'd be hard pressed to explain why she waited on a street corner alone for an unchaperoned ride with a man. Was she doing the right thing? The twisting of her stomach said no.

But even so, a small smile curved her lips. Though this was a mischievous charade, the forbidden excitement of taking tea with the man of her dreams pulsed through her. Was this how *Bleak House*'s heroine Ada Clare had felt when sneaking off to marry Richard Carstone?

Minutes later, a hansom cab rambled closer, and the jarvey pulled on the reins, stopping the carriage at the curb in front of her. It had to be Will, and though she knew it in her head, her heart still fluttered as he climbed out.

He studied her as he held the door open with one hand. "Mina, is that you?"

"Shh," she warned as she drew near, casting a look over her shoulder. Thankfully no one stood close enough to have heard her name. "Yes, it's me," she whispered.

He offered his hand and a brilliant smile. "Then shall we?"

His strong fingers wrapped around hers as he boosted her into the cab. Once they were both seated, he rapped on the roof, and the carriage lurched into motion.

Sitting this close to Will, she fixed her gaze straight ahead. One peek at him would only add to the jitters in her stomach. Simply breathing in the scent of his bergamot cologne and bumping into his shoulder upped her pulse.

"I understand your desire for disguise, but. . ." He tugged the hem of her veil. "Uncle Barlow might get the impression ours is not a happy marriage."

Leaning forward, she scanned the street to make sure none of the figures they passed looked even remotely familiar, then she sank back against the seat. "I suppose I could take it off now."

She lifted the lacy fabric from her head, then worked to tuck the veil into her reticule. The small pouch strained at the seams, and the drawstring fought against her as she tried to tighten it. Perhaps she ought to have made sure the head covering would fit inside her bag before she'd left home. What would William's relatives think of her with such a lump hanging from her arm?

"I appreciate you going along with me." The warmth in Will's voice stilled her hands. With him beside her, would it even matter what his relatives thought?

"I hope this meeting won't prove too uncomfortable for you," he continued.

She faced him, and her heart rocked every bit as much as the cab's wheels juddering over the cobbles. This close up, his eyes were bluer than she'd credited, like a sea without shores, endless and sparkling. Half a smile softened his clean-shaven jawline, and for the first time, she noticed a slight tilt to one of his front teeth—an endearing little flaw.

"Don't fret about me." She clutched the seat to keep from banging against him as the cab turned a corner. "If I can manage a taproom of clerks and solicitors, I am confident I can manage your uncle."

"That's the spirit." His grin faded, and he looked away. "Though it's not my uncle I am concerned about."

At least that's what it sounded like he said. Hard to tell the way he'd spoken under his breath. She leaned toward him, ears straining. "What was that?"

"Oh, er, I was just wondering. . ." Once again, his blue gaze met hers. "Have you been to Purcell's before?"

"Purcell's? Oh, my!" Immediately her hand shot to her hair, tucking in strays and straightening her bonnet. How often she'd fancied a visit to the famed literary haunt, rubbing shoulders with some of her favorite authors, and now she was to actually patronize such a place? Why was God so good to her?

Clenching every possible muscle to keep from bouncing on her seat in anticipation, she smiled at Will. "Do you think we might spy Mr. Dickens or Mr. Tennyson? Maybe even the Bells or Mr. Melville?"

"I doubt I should recognize any of the fellows you just mentioned."

Her smile faded a bit. "But surely you've heard of them?"

"No, not a one. Should I have?"

Her smile disappeared altogether. He seriously didn't know such august names? Did William Barlow not read? Her throat closed, and she swallowed back the lump clogging it. This was a definite chink in her hero's armor.

"Mina? Is something wrong?"

Alarm deepened his voice, and she determined not only to

forgive him for his ignorance but to introduce him to the wonders of literature as well. "No, nothing. That last bump didn't set well with my stomach, is all."

"Well, then thank goodness this ride is over"—the cab stopped—"for here we are."

Will opened the door and helped her out. While he paid off the jarvey, she forced the strap of her unwieldy reticule onto her wrist and looked up at the renowned establishment. Mist settled on her face and eyes, and she blinked so much it was hard to read the fancy name shingle with Purcell's painted in gilt.

"Let's get you out of this dreadful weather." Will offered his arm.

She wrapped her fingers around his sleeve and walked into heaven. Inside the large reception area, her feet sank into a thick Turkish carpet. Wall sconces flickered, and a massive overhead chandelier glittered light like fairy dust over all. Beyond the podium, where a concierge stood as a sort of gatekeeper, the drone of voices hummed. How many stories were being hatched even as she stood here? How many clever ideas? What kind of great minds fortified themselves with tea while working out plots and characters and all manner of epic tales?

Will approached the concierge. "The name is Barlow, meeting with a Mr. Charles Barlow."

The man ran his finger along a document. Halfway down, the motion stopped, and he looked up. "Ahh, yes. One moment, please."

As the man turned to summon a porter, the front door opened. A gust of wind howled in—accompanied by a woman's strident voice remarking on the excessive chill of the day.

"Well, well, look at this. William already here and on time, no less." A man's voice attacked them from behind. "My fine cousin appears to be all cleaned up and with a pretty little bauble on his arm. How on earth did you manage either of those two miracles?"

Beneath her touch, Will's muscles hardened to steel. He blew out a low breath, then winked at her. "I hope you're ready for this."

Without waiting for her response, he guided her around to face two scowls.

The woman in front of Mina was dressed head to toe in midnight blue and ornamented with an extravagant amount of black lace. Her blond hair was coiffed into a coil beneath a feathered hat and pierced through with a silver bodkin, as was all the rage. She was curvaceous, pretty, tall. All in all, quite striking.

Yet something wasn't right about the woman, giving Mina a queer feeling in her stomach. She edged nearer to Will. Nothing appeared untoward about the lady. Every button and thread was in place. No. . .it was more of an invisible atmosphere that clouded about her. A kind of foreboding. Like being alone in a big house and hearing a door slam—and knowing that something was coming for you.

Swallowing, Mina shifted her gaze to the man. He was shorter than the woman but every bit as snappily dressed in his dark grey suit with a white, high-stock collar. His round spectacles enlarged his eyes to dark marbles, and his black hair was pasted back with pomade. He might be a businessman. Or a lawyer. But the longer Mina stared, the more she suspected he might be better suited as an undertaker, so emotionless and coldly did he look upon her.

"Percy, Alice, good to see you." Will's voice strained on the word *good*.

The woman—Alice—sniffed as if he'd offered her a plate of rotted cabbage. "A pig in a suit does not a gentleman make, exemplified in your lack of introductions." Her head swiveled to Mina. "I am Alice Barlow, Percival's wife. And you are?"

Mina tensed. *These* were William's relatives? No wonder he spent most of his nights at the Golden Egg instead of taking part in family affairs.

Will placed his hand on the small of her back in a show of affection. "This is my. . .this is Mina."

Alice's upper lip twitched. "Mina? What sort of a name is that?"

"It's, uh. . ." Mouth suddenly dry as bones, Mina licked her lips, hoping to grease the way for more words to slip out. "It is the shortened form of Wilhelmina. My father's side of the family has Dutch roots."

"Oh." Alice said no more, but she didn't have to. The tone put Mina in her place—on a ladder rung clearly beneath Alice's jewel-toed shoes.

"Uncle mentioned you'd taken a wife." Percy's gaze drifted from Will to Mina. "My condolences."

Mina blinked. Were these people flesh and blood, or were they some of Mr. Dickens's villainous characters?

"Mr. Barlow," the concierge called out. "You may be seated now."

The man barely finished speaking before Percy and Alice shot into motion, nearly knocking her sideways were it not for Will's strong arm behind her. Her reticule swung wild, smacking into Alice as she passed—and earned Mina yet another glower.

Mina peered up at Will as his cousins disappeared through the door. "Are they always this way?" she whispered.

"No." A devilish grin tugged his lips. "Usually, they are worse."

But as she stepped into the grandeur of the tearoom, all thoughts of Will's cousins vanished. Walking beside her handsome prince, it was easy to pretend she was royalty. White linen tablecloths with fresh flowers adorned every table. Men and women of stature lifted dainty cakes to their lips or sipped from fine porcelain cups. The whole room twinkled as light shimmered off the gilded stripes on the pale blue wallpaper.

Slowly, the tight knots in her shoulders loosened, and she lifted her chin. This was where she wanted to belong, not slaving away in an inn that reeked of ale and grease. If she lived in such a world of opportunity and wealth, she could actually do something worthy with her life. Instead of scraping up saved coins to benefit the likes of the institute, she could give so much more. Do so much more. *Be* so much more, a benefactress that would really make a difference to others.

By the time they reached a table in the back corner, Will's cousins had already taken their seats, but yet standing was a thin fellow, dressed all in brown. White hair circled the man's head like a crown, tufting out at the sides near his ears. His face was a roadmap of years. Grey eyes—as piercing as Will's—twinkled with humour and something more. . .an innocence of sorts. As if, were the lines and grey hairs taken away, he might be naught more than a schoolboy looking for a good game of cricket.

"Uncle Barlow?" Will stared at the man. "Is it really you, sir?"

"Posh! Such formality. Of course it's me. Though I suppose I am quite a few stones lighter than when you last saw me." A cough rumbled in his chest, and he pulled out a handkerchief, holding it to his mouth until the spell passed.

Mina frowned. Will hadn't said anything about his uncle's frail health.

"Sorry." The man tucked the cloth back into his pocket with a wink reminiscent of Will's. "The past year has not been kind to me, but no cause for alarm. My doctor assures me I am on the mend. Now then." He pulled Will in for an embrace with a hearty pat on his back, then released him, chuckling. "This may be the first occasion you've ever arrived on time, my boy." His gaze swung toward her. "Surely you have wrought great miracles in my nephew."

She ought to answer him, truly, especially with the expectant tilt to his head, but her tongue fell flat. Facing this dear old man, posing as William's wife, suddenly stabbed her in the heart.

"Uncle," Will cut in, "allow me to introduce my. . .well, this is Mina. Mina, my uncle, Mr. Charles Barlow."

Uncle Barlow reached for her hand and bowed over it with a light kiss. "Welcome to the family, my dear. I look forward to getting to know you."

Her heart twisted, and she drew back her fingers. The old fellow would not say such things if he knew he held the hand of a deceiver.

She glanced over her shoulder, judging the distance to the door. She never should have agreed to this. Would Will forgive her if she dashed out of here now?

CHAPTER FIVE

There are strings. . .in the human heart
that had better not be vibrated.
Barnaby Rudge

Will tugged at his collar, despising the cravat choking his neck. Thank God this farce would soon be over. How could he have imagined this would work? He didn't have the slightest notion of how a husband should act, though he should have by now if Elizabeth hadn't—

He reached for his tea and slugged back a scalding mouthful, welcoming the burn. Anything to keep from remembering. He'd sworn to never again allow a woman access to his heart. What had possessed him to playact such a scene?

Beside him, Mina sipped her tea as she listened to one of Uncle's stories. Ahh, but she was a good sport and a true friend. Not to mention brave. He barely had the fortitude himself to sit here and endure Percy's remarks and Alice's thinly concealed glowers.

Across the table, Percy looked down his nose at him, a smug lift to one brow—the same look Will had received that Christmas years ago when, as lads, Percy had caught him with Uncle's snuffbox hidden behind his back. Percy never had been able to prove that he'd pinched a wad, but that hadn't stopped his cousin from trying.

Will snuck a covert glance over at Uncle Barlow. The old fellow seemed to be enjoying Mina, and he hadn't made one remark yet on Will's jaded past. At the very least, perhaps this tea would mend the relational fences Will had broken as a young fool. Even now, thinking of his past rebellious ways sickened him.

"Excuse me, Mina, is it?" Alice impaled Mina with a cancerous gaze. For a moment, she didn't speak, but twirled one finger around a silver locket. "What did you say your maiden name was?"

Mina, God bless her, smiled at the woman. "It is Scott."

"*Is?*" Alice's fingers froze midtwirl, and she lowered her hand.

Will tensed. A slip like that was enough rope in Alice's hand to string up Mina and hang her with her own words. He forced a small laugh. "You'll have to excuse Mina, for you see, the name Barlow is still so new to her."

"Speaking of which, how long have you—" Uncle set down his teacup and once again pulled out his handkerchief as another coughing spell overtook him.

Will frowned. Was Uncle Barlow truly getting better? Perhaps he ought to press the man to get a second opinion from a different doctor.

The hacking faded, and Uncle tucked his kerchief away. Leaning toward Mina, he smiled at her. "As I was saying, how long have you known my nephew, my dear?"

She exchanged a glance with Will before she answered. "Nearly a year."

"Really?" Percy's eyes narrowed. "That seems a rather whirlwind courtship from start to finish. How long did you say you've been married?"

"Tell me, Percy," Will cut in, hoping to divert the man. "I've been meaning to ask, has your bout of the itch cleared up yet?"

Red worked its way up Percy's neck. "I will thank you to keep my personal information to yourself."

Alice swung her gaze to Will, apparently impervious to her husband's distress. "At least your wife's former surname is not an unpronounceable bit of French twaddle like your mother's was."

Beneath the tablecloth, his hands curled into fists. He should've known his mother would have been shaken out and hung to dry at some point in today's conversation. She always was—which was why they could never know she was still alive. Working his jaw, he forced his tone to remain light. "My mother has nothing to do with this."

"I should think she does." Percy faced Uncle Barlow, nearly blinding them all as chandelier light reflected off his glasses. "Surely you would hate to see the wealth of your English forefathers tainted by someone with French blood."

"My husband is right." Alice sipped her tea as she eyed Uncle Barlow. "Percy has solid investments lined up with men who have bloodlines that go back to King Richard. Dear Uncle, there should be no more delay in getting your will and property signed over to Percy."

Uncle grunted, then drifted sideways toward Mina. " 'Something will come of this. I hope it mayn't be human gore.' "

She clapped her hands together with a laugh at Uncle Barlow's quotation. "Simon Tappertit is one of my favorite characters in *Barnaby Rudge*."

"Oh? A Dickens admirer, are you?" Uncle Barlow leaned back in his chair, surveying the breadth of the tearoom. "Look, there he goes now. Posh it! I should have liked to have introduced you."

Will followed his uncle's gaze to see a long-legged man in a houndstooth dress coat clap a bowler atop his head and stride out the door.

"You know Charles Dickens?"

The awe in Mina's voice drew his gaze back to her. She stared at Uncle, wide eyed and pink cheeked, respect and admiration radiating off her in waves. What would it feel like if she looked at Will so? His chest tightened. Even during their best moments, Elizabeth had never paid him such due.

"I should say so," Uncle answered. "Charles and I go way back. Let me tell you of the time—"

"Enough nattering of folderol." Percy clinked his teacup onto the saucer, jarring them all. "Back to the matter at hand."

"I agree." Picking up her napkin, Alice dabbed her lips, apparently finished with her refreshment and the whole conversation. "I see no reason to delay this affair."

"Especially since it appears you've already spent Uncle's money on some ridiculous investments," Will shot back.

"Why, I ought to—"

"Oh, pardon me. Did I say that aloud?"

"Listen, *Cousin*." Percy shot the word like a poison arrow. "You are unfit in every respect to inherit Uncle Barlow's estate. My wife is perfectly astute in her observation. I see no reason to postpone the paperwork whatsoever."

"Take a care, Cousin. You are dreadfully close to suffering an apoplexy." Will stifled a smile at the slight tremor rippling across Percy's shoulders. Truly, it was wicked of him to prod the man so, but ever so satisfying. Were Fitz here, he'd be rolling on the floor, laughing in spasms.

Alice gasped such a sharp intake, her corset strings were likely in danger of snapping. "I never! Such a lack of manners. Such ill-bred, uncouth—"

Soft laughter and a bass chuckle drew all their attention. Mina and Uncle Barlow conspired over their teacups like bosom companions, alternating between whispers and laughter.

Uncle wiped the moisture from his eyes with his knuckle. "William, you could not have married a more delightful young lady. I am pleased that you have mended your ways and become a man of honor. It seems you've taken full advantage of the second chance I offered you a year ago, and I couldn't be more proud."

Will's gut churned, and a sour taste filled his mouth. Those were exactly the words he'd hoped to hear, the sole reason for asking Mina to attend this tea. But now that the victory was his, he didn't want it. Not like this.

Averting his gaze, he hung his head. "Thank you, sir."

Alice blew out a snort. "Pish!"

Uncle Barlow held up a hand, cutting her off. "As you all know, I am soon to announce an heir for my estate, and I've given much thought to it these past months. Therefore, I should like to name—"

Will looked up. Alice and Percy leaned so far toward Uncle, their chairs might go under at any moment. Even Mina quieted.

"—a date two weeks hence," Uncle continued. "Yes, in exactly a fortnight, I think. We shall meet over dinner the Thursday following next at my townhouse. Eight o'clock. Is this agreeable?"

"Yes." Will's voice chimed in unison with his cousins', offset by Mina's, "No."

Will draped his arm around Mina's shoulder, ignoring the tension his touch created. "Mina is right. We should first check our calendar. Yes, my sweet?" He gave her a little squeeze.

And a sharp kick jabbed him in the leg. The little firebrand. He drew back his hand.

"Well, well, William. I must say I am impressed with such forethought." Uncle Barlow stroked his jaw. "You will let me know at your earliest convenience, will you not?"

"Of course," he said before Mina could speak.

Ignoring the sneers on his cousins' faces, he blew out a long breath. That crisis had been averted, but he'd soon face an even bigger one—what to do about the dinner in two weeks.

Chapter Six

Accidents will occur in the best regulated families.

David Copperfield

Dinner. Two weeks. In a fine London townhouse.

Uncle Barlow's invitation sank to Mina's stomach like one too many biscuits. As much as she was growing to like the man, there was no way she could attend. All the bright beauty of taking tea at Purcell's faded as she glanced at Will. How she hated to disappoint him, but stealing away for an hour in the afternoon was altogether different from being gone an entire evening for hours on end. And now that she'd met his dear uncle, the thought of continuing their charade pricked her conscience.

The touch of Uncle Barlow's hand atop hers pulled her gaze back to the old fellow, and her heart twisted at the affection shining in his grey eyes. Will's uncle reminded her far too much of her grandfather, God rest his soul. Grandfather had been the only man to understand her love affair with literature...until now.

"It has been a delight to meet you, my dear. I look forward to seeing you again." Uncle Barlow leaned closer, speaking for her alone. "When 'all the knives and forks were working away at a rate that was quite alarming; very few words were spoken; and everybody seemed to eat his utmost in self-defense, as if a famine were expected to set in before breakfast.'" He reared back in his seat and challenged her with a tip of his chin. "Can you name that one?"

She couldn't stop the smile that stretched her lips. "*Martin Chuzzlewit.*"

Uncle Barlow's shoulders shook with a great chuckle. "Ahh, but you do a heart good." Then he pressed his hands on the tabletop and stood. "And now, I bid you all adieu."

Their chairs scraped back as one. "Good day, Uncle Barlow," she said along with Will.

But Percy and Alice immediately swarmed the man, hooking their arms through his. "We shall be glad to escort you to the door."

"No need." He shrugged them off. "I may have a cough, but I am not feeble."

Collecting his cane, he threaded his way through the tables and disappeared out the door.

Will offered Mina his arm, then squared off with Percy. "Until next time, Cousin."

Percy scowled. "Indeed."

As she and Will crossed to the door, Mina memorized every last inch of the tearoom, for she'd revisit it in daydreams to come. In the foyer, Will helped her into her coat, and when they stepped outside, she left Purcell's behind feeling a curious mix of lightness and heaviness. That she'd have to tell Will she couldn't attend the dinner weighed her down. So did the thought of the disapproval in Uncle Barlow's eyes when he discovered the truth.

But regardless, as she stood next to Will while he hailed a cab, she couldn't stop from curving her lips upward. It had been lovely to be a lady for an afternoon, so much so that if it weren't improper, she would have thrown up her arms and twirled. . .but wait a minute. Her gaze shot to her arm—which lacked an overly stuffed reticule.

"Oh!" She laid her fingers on Will's coat sleeve. "I'm afraid I left my bag back at the table."

"Not to worry. I'll retrieve it in a trice—"

"No." She shook her head. "I'll dash off. You hail a cab. If I stay any later, Father will get suspicious."

Will's brow crumpled, but at last he consented. "Very well."

Turning on her heel, she darted back into Purcell's and stopped at the concierge stand. "I'm sorry, but I believe I left my bag at the table."

"It may have been cleared by now," the fellow answered. "Yet you are free to take a look."

Murmuring a thank-you, she hurried into the tearoom, trying not to look conspicuous as she rushed to the table in the rear corner. But the dishes had been removed. A new cloth awaited the setting of a fresh tea set, and no black knit bag sat beneath the chair where she'd laid it.

She pursed her lips. *Oh, bother.* Though the small pouch contained only her veil and no money, still, it was a good veil. Her only one. And she'd be sorry to lose it.

Retracing her steps, she worked her way to the side of the large chamber, where she'd have a straight shot back to the foyer. She'd barely made it when Percy and Alice appeared from the necessary rooms. Drat! Facing them with Will at her side had been hard enough. Alone she was no match. In two clipped steps, she flattened behind a large potted plant, using the greenery for cover.

As Will's cousins drew close, Alice's voice traveled a layer above the din of tea chatter. "There is no time to waste, especially if your uncle is to name the heir in two weeks. You must line up an appointment with the doctor and the administrator."

"Yes, of course." Percy grumbled. "Once the paperwork is signed, I'll make sure Uncle goes the way of Aunt Prudence. Though William will no doubt put up a fuss once he finds out."

"That is a problem. . .but what if he doesn't hear of it? What if we simply lead him to believe your uncle is retiring to his country estate? William hasn't visited there in years. I don't see why he should start now."

"He might, now that he's got a wife."

Their voices started to fade, and Mina wavered. It was wicked to eavesdrop, but judging by what she'd already heard, Will's cousins meant some kind of harm to Uncle Barlow—harm that perhaps she could prevent. Edging away from the plant, she angled her ear to catch the last drift of their conversation as they moved toward the foyer.

Alice snorted. "Then we'll tell your cousin that Uncle isn't feeling up to company. Something about his cough or other such tale. Besides, once your uncle is committed to an asylum, he won't last long. We'll be the owners of the estate, and Will and his bride can go to kingdom come."

"You are delightfully devious, my dear."

Alice's purr disappeared with her out the door, leaving Mina behind with a pounding heart and a righteous anger. Will's cousins didn't just want Uncle Barlow's money. They wanted to destroy him.

And in the worst possible way.

CHAPTER SEVEN

The plain rule is to do nothing in the dark,
to be a party to nothing underhanded or mysterious,
and never to put his foot where he cannot see the ground.
Bleak House

Sneaking a covert look into the foyer to make sure Will's cousins were gone—and finding it empty—Mina dashed out of the tearoom.

"Miss!" The porter's voice stopped her retreat.

She stared at the reticule sitting on his upturned palm, but all she could think of were Will's horrible cousins and their threat to Uncle Barlow. Would they truly shut the old fellow away? And if they did, how long could he possibly last?

"Is this your bag, madam?"

The man's question rattled her from her dark thoughts, and she reached for the black pouch. "It is, and I thank you."

Without another word, she whirled and dashed out to where Will waited at the side of a cab.

He offered his hand to help her step up, then looked closer at her face. "Are you all right? You look as if you've. . .hold on. Did you have to square off with Percy and Alice?" He shook his head. "I should've gone to retrieve your bag. Forgive me?"

She frowned. If only it were something so trivial. "There is nothing to forgive," she murmured.

Clutching his hand, she desperately tried to figure out how to tell Will all she'd overheard. She settled her skirts on the cab's seat, trying not to inhale overmuch. It was going to be a long ride home in a hackney that reeked of sardines and cigar smoke. As Will climbed in and shut the door, not even his pleasant bergamot scent could beat back the rank odor—or stop the sickening twist of her heart. Poor Uncle Barlow.

As soon as the cab rolled onward, she turned to Will.

But his words came out first. "Thank you, Mina, for everything. I daresay my uncle is completely smitten with you."

A small smile trembled across her lips, for the feeling had been completely mutual. Not only had the old fellow quoted from some of her favorite books, but he also kept company with authors she longed to meet. "Your Uncle Barlow is a dear old man. I see where you get your good humour. But there's something I must tell you."

He humphed. "Would that Percy might have gotten a smidgen of Uncle's humour as well, hmm?"

She bit her lip, stopping the agreement from flying from her lips. Will's friend Mr. Fitzroy couldn't have been more right when he'd deemed the fellow a pompous donkey.

"Come on." Will nudged her with his elbow. "Admit it. My cousin is an odious beast."

"Your words, not mine."

"Yet you thought so, did you not?"

"Well. . .I do not normally like to speak ill of people, but there is something—"

"Something?" His brows rose. "That's putting it mildly. There's far more than something wrong with Percy. Since we were children, he's done nothing but browbeat me or anyone else who crosses his path. A learned trait, I suppose, from his father. But you, Mina," his voice softened. "You were a terribly good sport about the whole thing. Still, I am thankful it's over. I'll never expose you to Percy or Alice again."

"But what about the dinner?"

"I'm not sure yet, but I'll have a few days to figure it out. At the very least, I could say you simply weren't feeling up to attending, which wouldn't be a huge stretch, for Lord knows even I never feel up to rubbing elbows with Percy."

"But I—"

"No buts about it. I cannot ask you to do more. You've been a good friend."

Friend? Oh, how she wished to be so much more. The cab clattered along and her darker thoughts returned, rattling her as much as the jarring ride. Would her lack of appearance at that dinner cause Uncle Barlow to name Percy his heir? And if Percy were named. . .she shuddered as his words surfaced in her mind.

"Once the paperwork is signed, I'll make sure Uncle goes the way of Aunt Prudence."

"Will." She shifted on the seat and faced him. "Tell me what happened to your aunt Prudence."

His eyes narrowed. "How on earth do you know her name? Did Uncle mention something about her?"

"No. I overheard Percy and Alice speaking of her when I went back to find my reticule."

"Did you?" A glower shadowed his face, and suddenly the cheerful man she adored vanished. "What did they say?"

Plagued by a sudden bout of nerves, she licked her lips. Did he think ill of her for eavesdropping, or had the mention of his cousins darkened his brow?

"Alice said something about paperwork being signed and your uncle going the way of Aunt Prudence. I pray I am wrong on my assumptions, but I must know. What happened to your aunt?"

Lightning flashed in Will's eyes, and she edged back—which was a trifling distance in a cab of this size.

"What is it?" she whispered.

"My aunt Prudence," he gritted out, "was committed to an asylum. At the time, Uncle Barlow acted on advice from her physician. Yet she was horribly mistreated in the name of medical science, and by the time he finished the paperwork to have her released, well. . . it was too late."

Breathe. Just breathe. But no good. Though Mina tried to ignore them, ghosts from the past rose up and squeezed the air from her lungs. She flung out her hand to grip the side of the cab.

"Mina? Are you ill?"

She trained her gaze on him, slowly bringing him into focus until she could shake the memory of voices screeching to her from across the years. "You *cannot* allow anyone to put your uncle into an asylum," she said finally. "You must go to him and reveal what your cousins are plotting."

He assessed her in silence for a long moment, his jaw grinding the whole while. "I don't think Uncle Barlow will believe me. My reputation is not pretty in his eyes. He'll see the attempt as nothing but a scheme to put Percy out of the running."

She jerked sideways to face him, dropping her reticule and spilling her veil onto the cab's floor. How was she to make Will realize how important it was for him to take a stand against such an atrocity? "You must try! Your uncle's life may depend upon it."

Will stared at her, and only God knew what went on behind those blue eyes of his, now turned to ice. Had she said too much? Been too forceful? Crossed some sort of line she ought not have?

He bent and retrieved her belongings, taking time to brush off a bit of mud from the veil before handing it back. "Trust me, Mina." His voice was low and weighted with a burden she couldn't begin to comprehend. "I understand the severity of the situation. My cousins would only deny it should I bring the charge against them. Scraps of overheard whispers are insufficient evidence in a court of law."

She sank back against the seat, clutching her bag. He was right of course, but that was no comfort. Slowly, she smoothed out the wrinkles in her veil, then forced a steadiness to her voice that she didn't feel. "Do you not believe me?"

"Nothing of the sort. I know better than most the deviousness of Percy's character. Blast it!" Lifting his hat, he raked his fingers through his hair. "I need proof, Mina. If I hope to convince Uncle Barlow of Percy's intent, I'll need something more concrete than mere hearsay."

"But if your cousins succeed and put your uncle into an asylum, he won't survive. The cures used in the name of medicine are enough to kill a healthy person. You heard your uncle's cough. Shutting him away in a drafty institution would be the end of him."

Will's hands curled into fists on his thighs, so unlike his amiable self. "I know," he breathed out.

She heaved a sigh herself. Of course he'd need something more valid than what she'd overheard. But how else could his cousins be stopped?

The cab slowed, and she pressed her hand to the door, as though by so doing, she could delay her decision. She met Will's gaze, afraid to hope—yet more afraid not to. "Do you think. . .is there a chance your Uncle Barlow will name you heir at his dinner?"

Will scrubbed his hand over his face. "As much as I'd like to say yes, the truth is I do not know."

"Are there any other options if Percy is your uncle's choice? You are a law clerk. Are there not statutes in place to prevent such a heinous act?"

"None." His mouth twisted into a rueful smile. "I'm afraid the legal system is in need of an overhaul in more than one way."

Why did everything seem to be against that dear old man? She shoved open the door, debating what to do all the while, then faced Will. Icy rain pelted in from outside, and she shivered, though less from the chill than from her decision. "Well then, we will just have to make sure your uncle chooses you over Percy at that dinner."

Will's jaw dropped, and for a moment no words came out. "You... you want to go through with this?"

She lifted the veil and covered her face, then clutched her reticule with a death grip.

"We must do everything we can to keep your uncle from being committed to an asylum. No one should ever have to suffer what my mother did."

Chapter Eight

These sequestered nooks are the public offices of the legal
profession, where writs are issued, judgments signed,
declarations filed, and numerous other ingenious machines
put in motion for the torture and torment
of His Majesty's liege subjects.
The Pickwick Papers

Will stared at the stack of documents in his hands, but he didn't
see them. All he could focus on was the haunted glaze in
Mina's eyes as she'd run out of the cab yesterday. A look so ripe
with heartbreak and sorrow, he'd wanted to pull her into his arms
and protect her from it—and that was a feeling so new and foreign
he still didn't know what to do with it. Thunderation! He never
should have allowed Uncle Barlow to believe he was married. What
a tangled web he'd woven.

Giving himself a mental shake, he reached for the bell on his
desk and rang it. No sense dwelling on what couldn't be made
right—not yet, anyway. As he waited for a runner to leave the clus-
ter of other errand boys near the door, he determined to go to the
Golden Egg as soon as the workday was over and put a smile back
onto Mina's face. It was the least he could do for having troubled
her with his family affairs.

Satisfied with his plan of action, he tucked the papers into a
courier bag and inhaled his first relaxed breath of the morning. The
Temple Court clerks' room hummed with quiet activity. Papers
shuffled. Pen nibs scritch-scratched like little feet running across

so many pages, and the hushed whispers of conferring clerks circled the room, as dry and rustling as leaves caught up in an eddy.

A ruddy-cheeked lad, flat cap set low on his brow, approached his desk with his hand out. "Where to, sir?"

"Barrister Dalrymple, King's Court Chambers." He started to hand over the packet, when Thomas Fitzroy reached out and snatched it away.

"Are you out of your mind?" Fitz rumbled, garnering a black look from the clerk seated a row ahead.

"Are you out of yours?" Will whispered back. "This Jarndyce brief needs to get to Barrister Dalrymp—"

He stiffened. Great heavens! Fitz was right. He'd nearly sent the paperwork to the wrong barrister.

"Thank you, Charlie. That will be all for now." Fitz dismissed the runner with a nod of his head, then frowned down at Will. "What's going on? That's the third error you've made in the past hour, and this one could have cost you your job."

"I know. I...well...it's complicated." He laced his hands behind his head and looked up at Fitz—his true friend. His only friend, really, since his fall from grace.

"Complicated?" Fitz snorted. "It always is with you. Let's have it."

Will shoved back his stool. Perhaps his friend had a useful thought or two on his current conundrum, for if nothing else, Fitz always had an opinion. "Very well. Come along."

He wove past their fellow clerks, beyond a wall lined with bookshelves, then skirted the collection of runners waiting for the chance to deliver documents. Out in the corridor, he stopped halfway down and leaned against the wall.

Fitz pulled up alongside of him, practically bouncing on his toes. "I can't wait to hear this. What is it that has you so befuddled?"

"Remember that tea I told you about, the one Mina Scott agreed to attend with me?"

For a moment, Fitz's brows drew into a line, then suddenly

lifted. "Ahh. That's right. I completely forgot to ask you about it. I'm afraid it was a late night for me with the King's Court boys last evening." He winced and massaged his temple with two fingers. "How did it go?"

Before Will answered, he listed aside and scanned the passageway beyond Fitz's shoulders. The walls of Temple Court contained an overzealous penchant for gossip—and he'd rather not provide fodder for this week's feast. Thankfully this early in the day, most clerks were still readying their papers for delivery, and none lurked about here. Even so, he lowered his voice. "Not good at all. Uncle Barlow's life is in peril if my cousin Percy gets his hands on the old man's estate. Mina overheard Percy threaten to have Uncle committed to an asylum should he be named heir."

A growl rumbled in Fitz's throat. "Your cousin always was a conniving cur."

"Indeed. And unless I convince Uncle that I am the more deserving beneficiary, there will be nothing I can do to stop him. Knowing Percy, he's likely already got a physician in his pocket, ready to sign whatever papers are needed to have my uncle committed."

"Hmm." Fitz folded his arms. "Then we'll have to fill your pocket as well."

He narrowed his eyes. "What do you mean?"

"Even if what you say is true, and your cousin has people in place, that shouldn't stop you from finding other people to counteract his devious plan. Perhaps there is a loophole in the committal process that can be found. Or maybe there's some kind of reversal application, or well, I don't know. But I do know someone who would. Old Kenwig's the man for you."

Kenwig? Of course. He should have thought of the elderly barrister himself. The man was more ancient than half the laws on the books. Will rolled his shoulders, the tension in his muscles already loosening. "Is he in today?"

"Only one way to find out. Go on." Fitz clouted him on the

back. "I'll look over that Jarndyce brief while you're at it."

"Thanks. I owe you one." He took off down the passage.

And Fitz's voice followed. "I'll be sure to cash in on that. Tonight. The Golden Egg."

Will trotted up the stairway. The corridor at the top was far better decorated than that to which the clerks were delegated. His shoes sank into a rug instead of thudding against wooden planks, and light glimmered from brass sconces, not tin. This was a world of silks, not woolens—the world of wealth Elizabeth had aspired to. . .and won.

Shoving down bitter memories, he strode the length of the corridor, and found the door to Barrister Kenwig's receiving room open. A good sign, that. He entered, expecting to persuade Kenwig's personal attendant for an interview with a smile and a coin, if need be. But the tall desk inside and the stool behind it sat empty. Beyond that, the door to the barrister's inner chamber yawned open. Perhaps the clerk had ducked in to have a word with the old man. Will stepped nearer, straining to listen, but no conversation drifted out. Emboldened, he strode to the threshold and peeped in.

On the other side of a massive desk sat a bulwark of the English legal system. Barrister Kenwig lifted a document in one gnarled hand and a magnifying glass in the other—making one eye appear larger than life, slightly milky but bearing keen intelligence. He wore his wrinkles like a garment, the deep creases on his face in sore need of a good ironing. Though the morning was well advanced, he hadn't yet donned his black silk robe.

Will rapped on the doorframe, thankful the man hadn't left for court already. "Pardon me, Barrister. I wonder if I might have a word?"

Kenwig lowered the magnifier and squinted at him. "Ahh, young Master Barlow. Come in. I can spare a few moments."

"Thank you, sir." He crossed the length of the chamber, inhaling the scent of musty books and beeswax, and as he drew nearer the man, breathed in an underlying odor of mothballs. He sank into the leather high-back in front of the barrister's desk. "I shall be brief. There is a hypothetical situation I was discussing with another clerk, one on which I should like your counsel."

"Very well." Kenwig reclined, his chair creaking—or maybe his bones. Hard to tell.

Will leaned forward. "Let's say an elderly gentleman who's never sired children of his own signs over his estate to another relation. This potential heir is a deviant at heart and has the old man committed to an asylum, thereby effectively taking possession of the man's money before he is deceased. And this brings me to my question. Is there any way to counteract or reverse that committal before it's been completely processed?

The barrister's gaze drifted toward the ceiling, as if an answer might be found in the carved plaster moulding. The mantel clock ticked, and the coals in the grate sank, but Kenwig said nothing.

Nor did Will. He'd learned long ago the best route with the old fellow was to allow him to roam the long corridors of his learned mind.

At length, Kenwig's gaze lowered to his. "Not before it's been processed, but afterward, there are two ways. Discharge of a patient can be initiated by the medical superintendent or at the request of the family."

"Truly?" He stifled a laugh. All he'd have to do was file counter-paperwork? Thank God! A smile twitched his lips.

"It appears this was not so hypothetical after all, hmm?" The barrister tapped a bony finger atop his desk. "Do not tell me you're the deviant, Mr. Barlow."

"No, sir." He glanced back at the door, on the off chance the attendant had returned. The threshold remained empty, but he scooted to the edge of his chair and tempered his tone. "It is my cousin, sir, though he's not yet officially been named heir. I may still have a chance at that. But if not, at least I know that I would be able to get my uncle released with a simple request."

Far lighter in spirit than when he'd first entered the chamber, Will stood and dipped his head in a respectful bow. "Thank you for your time, Barrister, and your sage wisdom. A very good day to you."

"Oh, Mr. Barlow." The old fellow lifted his finger. "One more thing."

Will paused, trying to ignore the foreboding twinge in his gut. "Yes, sir?"

"I should mention that while a discharge can be initiated by you, there is no guarantee it shall be granted. That kind of paperwork also needs the signature of the parish magistrate."

"That shouldn't be a problem. Should it?"

The barrister's thin shoulder lifted in a shrug. "Deviancy is not limited to unscrupulous family members. Tell me, what parish are we speaking of?"

"My uncle's townhouse is in St. James. His estate, in Harlow."

"Hmm." The word vibrated through the room like a faraway roll of thunder.

"Sir?"

"Well, I suppose it would depend upon where the paperwork is drawn up. I cannot speak for Harlow, as I am not well versed in the ethics of Essex law keepers, but I can tell you that the St. James magistrate is not known for his stalwart morals. I've heard rumours he is a man for hire. Tell me, Mr. Barlow, on the off chance the Harlow magistrate is of the persuadable variety, who has deeper pockets, you or your cousin?"

Blast! His fingers curled into fists. If Percy inherited, he'd have the larger purse—and the upper hand.

CHAPTER NINE

In a word, I was too cowardly to do what I knew
to be right, as I had been too cowardly to
avoid doing what I knew to be wrong.
Great Expectations

Mina strolled down Whitewell Street with her friend Effie Gedge. A brisk November wind pushed her from behind. But even so, her steps slowed as she neared the spot where she'd fled from the cab that rainy afternoon a week ago now—*before* Will could ask about her mother. A heroine would've given him some kind of explanation instead of running off like a coward. Oh, what a humbling truth.

Next to her, Effie rattled on about something, but it was hard to focus on her friend's words with so much guilt muddling her thoughts. Will had stopped by the Golden Egg the day after the tea, and the day after that. . .and, well, every day. But she'd avoided any sort of detailed conversation with him. The questions in his eyes ran too deep and many. She never should have mentioned her mother. Though she'd been hardly more than seven years old when Mother had died, it was a memory she didn't often revisit and rarely shared with anyone. What was the point of lifting a rock and staring horrified at the creepy-crawlies beneath?

Oh, Mother. What would it be like to have a soft shoulder to share her burdens with instead of a father who could think of nothing other than the upcoming Christmas Eve party or how to marry her off? She heaved a long, low breath. She'd never know, she supposed, and that was a perpetual ache.

Effie threaded her arm through hers. "That's the fifth time ye've sighed since we left the ribbon shop, love."

She matched her pace to Effie's and glanced sideways at her friend. "Hmm?"

"Have ye heard a word I've said?"

"Of course. You were saying how Mrs. Lane's new babe is the most adorable thing you've ever seen."

Effie frowned. "That was *before* the ribbon shop."

"Then you remarked on how exceptionally attentive Mr. Lane is to his wife and new son."

"That was *inside* the ribbon shop."

"Then you said that baby Benjamin is the sweetest thing ever and. . .er. . .something more about your employer." She released Effie's arm and lifted her skirts to avoid the mud. Effie followed suit, and they parted ways to maneuver around a puddle.

As soon as they drew together on the other side, Effie rummaged in her reticule and pulled out an old coin, then reached for Mina's hand and dropped it into her palm.

What on earth? Mina lifted the piece of gold to eye level. The edges were jagged in a few places. On one side, a big *X*—or maybe a cross—was embossed. Hard to tell for the wear. How many fingers had rubbed against this bit of metal? The other side sported foreign words, circling the perimeter, unlike any she'd ever seen. "What is this?"

"A second-chance coin. 'Twas once given to me by Mrs. Lane."

"A what?" She scrunched up her nose at her friend.

"Why, I'm giving ye a second chance, love."

She studied her friend's face. Brown eyes the colour of a stout cup of tea peered back at her. What was Effie going on about? Maybe she should have been paying closer attention. "For what exactly do I need a second chance?"

"To tell me what's really on yer mind." A passing dray lumbered by, nearly drowning out Effie's words with its grinding wheels. Her friend stepped nearer. "Ye've not been yourself the entire hour we've been together, and ye've very nicely danced around all my questions. I haven't much time remaining a'fore I must return to Mrs. Lane with this new lace." She patted her small parcel. "So, ye best talk fast, my friend."

The coin warmed against her skin, yet she wasn't so sure she wanted a second chance to reveal the snarly mess inside her head and heart. Still. . .it would be a release of sorts. And she hadn't a truer friend than Effie. She wrapped her fingers tight around the coin for strength. "Very well, but you mustn't breathe a word of this to anyone. Not to Miss Whymsy and especially not to Miss Minton, for she'd 'hear, hear' it all over town. Promise?"

Effie nodded, more solemn than the Reverend Mr. Graves on a Sunday morning. "Upon my word."

Mina tugged her friend aside, pulling her close to the glass window of Truman's Tinctures and Powders, well out of the path of pedestrians or curious ears. Even so, she lowered her voice so only Effie might hear. "You know that patron I've remarked on a few times over the past year?"

"If ye're speaking of the dashing Mr. Barlow, your figuring is way off. Few? Pah!" Effie chuckled. "If I only had a farthing for each time you sang the praises of the man, I'd be wealthy as a—"

"You see?" Mina cut her off with a glower. "This is why I haven't told you anything, for you can't manage to keep from teasing."

"All right." Effie's mouth rippled as she tried to stifle her grin. "I promise. Not another word."

With a glance past Effie's shoulder, she scanned the lane. Several men strode past on long legs, each carrying a paper-wrapped parcel. A stoop-shouldered lady in black shambled by, leaning heavily on a cane. Yet no one appeared to take an interest in her or Effie, so she faced her friend. "Mr. Barlow asked me to attend a tea with him and his uncle. That's why I had to ask to change our society meeting time last week."

"Aha! When you slipped out o' there like a wisp o' the breeze, I knew something weren't right." Effie arched a brow. "Will you soon be going the way of Mary Bowman then?"

"Of course not." But the thought of such pulsed through her. Despite the shortcomings she'd started to detect in Will, to be his true wife instead of a faux was a dream she wasn't yet willing to depart with.

"His interest in me isn't like that," she continued. "Mr. Barlow is in line to receive an inheritance from his uncle, especially if his Uncle Barlow believes him to be happily married and settled down."

"And you went"—Effie's eyes widened—"as his bride?"

"I did. And my! How grand it was." She closed her eyes, reliving the magnificence of Purcell's—until Will's cousins' faces surfaced, along with their threat against Uncle Barlow. Her eyelids popped open. "Well, it was mostly all grand, except for Will's awful cousins. Oh, Effie, they are conspiring to commit the dear old man to an asylum."

Speaking the words aloud breathed life into the monstrous possibility, squeezing her heart. "And you know as well as I what might happen to him there—" Her voice cracked, and she pressed her lips tight.

"There, there, love." Effie patted her arm. "I know that's a blow, considering yer mum—God rest her. But what can ye do?"

"That's just it. There is something I can do to help, but I'm not sure it's the right thing." She heaped another sigh onto her accumulating pile. "Uncle Barlow has invited us all to his townhouse for dinner next week. For the sake of William getting that inheritance, and thereby sparing his uncle from such a fate, I agreed to go. Apparently Uncle Barlow will only see fit to award his estate to an heir who's firmly rooted in faith *and* family. I am Will's family, of sorts, leastwise in Uncle Barlow's eyes. But how shall I tell Father? He'll never allow me to attend, especially if he discovers I am posing as Will's bride. Yet if I don't go, then Will's cousin might very well become the heir. . .and Will's uncle would be committed. It seems there is no good solution."

"Hmm," Effie murmured. "That is a dilemma."

The door to Truman's swung open, and both of them fell silent until the woman exiting strolled past them.

"I've got it." Effie beamed. "Why don't ye and Mr. Barlow simply go to his uncle and tell him the truth? If ye reveal the cousins' wicked plot, why, his uncle is sure to name your Will as heir and be glad of it."

Her Will? The idea of William Barlow belonging to her alone quickened her breath—but now was definitely not the time for fanciful dreaming. She shook her head. "I said as much to Mr. Barlow, but he thinks we need more evidence than a snippet of overheard conversation."

"He might be right, I suppose." Effie pinched the bridge of her nose, and Mina desperately hoped the action would coax out some golden wisdom for her to follow. But Effie merely lowered her hand and angled her head. "Ye'll just have to tell yer father the truth of things, love."

She sighed—again. If she kept this up, she'd have no air whatsoever left in her lungs. "I was afraid you'd say that."

"Mina." Compassion infused her friend's tone, far warmer than the November chill working its way into her bones. "Ye didn't really need me to tell ye what to do, eh?"

"Yes—I mean no. I mean. . .I suppose not." Shoving back another sigh, she straightened her shoulders. Effie was right. Deep down in her gut she'd known the correct course of action but, until now, had been trying to ignore it. And that's what she loved most about her friend. Effie had a magical way of giving her the courage to look within and dare to hold hands with what she knew to be right.

She lifted her chin, then grabbed for her hat as a brisk breeze nearly lifted it off her head. "You're right. I shall go to Father at once and explain the situation. If he allows me to attend the dinner for the sake of Mr. Barlow's uncle, then I shall. If not, well, either way I must leave this in God's hands."

Effie grinned. "I knew ye'd do the right thing. Shall I come along?"

"No. I fear I've made you late enough as is. Thank you, my friend, and I'll let you know how things turn out." She whirled to go, then as suddenly turned back. "Oh, I nearly forgot."

With a heavy heart, she retrieved a small purse containing all her savings for Father's watch fob. Though she tried to smile as she held it out, her lips didn't quite cooperate. "Here is my donation to the Institute for the Care of Sick Gentlewomen. I thought you might add it along with yours and see that Miss Whymsy gets it."

Effie eyed her as she collected the offering. "I suspect this is costing you more than some coins."

"It is." She nodded toward the pouch. "That was my sole funding to purchase Father a new fob for Christmas."

"Ahh, love." Effie shoved the purse back toward her. "Surely betwixt the two of us, we can come up with some other way to help the institute."

"I have thought of another way, for the fob, that is. Would you stop over when you've some free time and help me cut my hair? As inconspicuously as possible. I plan to fashion a braided twist for Father to use. It won't be as dashing as a gold chain, but it will be better than none."

Tucking the pouch into her pocket, Effie then straightened her shoulders and saluted. "My scissors are at yer command."

"Oh! One more thing." She held out her other hand, offering back Effie's second-chance coin on her open palm. "Here is your coin."

Effie curled Mina's fingers back around the gold piece. "I'll see yer contribution gets to Miss Whymsy, but you keep that coin. Tuck it in a pocket and carry it with you every day. When the right situation happens along, I'm sure ye'll know just when to use it. And in the meantime, when ere yer fingers rub against the metal, think on more than just the second chance I gave you. Think on the second chance God gives us all, eh love? Now, off with ye."

"Thank you, my friend. I shall see you next week." Turning on her heel, Mina tucked the coin into her reticule, then dashed down the lane faster than decorum allowed. But it was not to be helped. If she didn't get this over with soon, she might lose the pluck to tell her father.

At this time of the afternoon, only a few patrons sat with mugs in hand inside the taproom. It was the off-hour, the lull she would've taken advantage of to sneak off with her book if Father hadn't confiscated it again. At this rate, she'd never finish *David Copperfield*.

She strode directly to his office and rapped on the door before pushing it open. "Father?"

Behind his paper-strewn desk, Father's chair sat empty. Neither did the sweet scent of Cavendish tobacco waft in the air.

Shutting the door behind her, she dashed to the kitchen. Perhaps he indulged in a bite of one of Martha's meat pies.

"Father?" She swung into the kitchen and stopped inches in front of Martha.

"Peas and honey!" The cook retreated a step, a sprinkling of flour taking flight from her collar at the sudden movement. "Take a care, child."

"My apologies." She offered the woman a sheepish smile, all the while knowing it was a poor show of contrition. "I am looking for my father. Have you seen him?"

Martha swiped the back of her hand across her cheek, leaving behind a dusty smear. "He's gone."

"What do you mean, gone?"

"La, child!" Cook's lower lip folded. "Don't tell me ye've forgotten what day it is. Yer father left not an hour ago for his annual trip to Colchester to find this year's best oyster seller. Can't rightly have his famous stew for the Christmas Eve party if he don't have the best oysters."

"Oh, dear," she breathed out. She'd been so caught up in her own worries she hadn't given a second thought to the date—or Father's party preparations.

"Now, now. 'Tain't all that bad. He'll be back in little over a fortnight." A stray hair escaped from Martha's cap, and she blew the rogue away. She edged a step nearer, lowering her voice. "I suppose you should know, though, that your father arranged for Mr. Grimlock to come by on the morrow to manage things while he's absent."

Mr. Grimlock? She stiffened.

"Thank you, Martha," she forced out, then spun away before the cook could read the disgust that surely coloured her cheeks. Now not only would she not be able to tell Father about the dinner at Uncle Barlow's, but she'd have to dodge Gilbert Grimlock's perpetual advances. The man had proposed to her twice already. Of all the men Father could have chosen to tend the inn for him, it had to be Gilbert Grimlock? She narrowed her eyes.

Or had Father chosen the man on purpose as part of his never-ending scheme to marry her off?

CHAPTER TEN

The civility which money will purchase
is rarely extended to those who have none.
Sketches by Boz

Mina pressed her back against the corridor wall before she reached the kitchen, shrinking farther into the shadows as Gilbert Grimlock strode out the door. *Please don't come this way. Please don't even look.*

She'd spent the better part of the past week dodging the fellow. Despite her efforts, he'd occasionally caught her off guard. Such had been the case earlier today. After suffering a morning of the man's ego and innuendoes, she'd begged off with a headache. Which was no lie. His thinly veiled talk of marriage and continual boasting of his accomplishments never failed to throb in her temples.

Just past the threshold, Mr. Grimlock paused, the great hulk of him a dark, unmoving blob. She froze. What would she say if he turned back around and found her skulking about in her finest dress when he thought her abed? *Think. Think!*

But as unexplainably as he stopped, he once again set off, creeping toward the taproom like a giant spider.

She waited until he disappeared, and her crazed heartbeat slowed. Pushing away from the wall, she padded the rest of the way down the passage and slipped into the kitchen. Thankfully, Martha bent over a pot on the hearth, humming a folk tune and stirring up a frenzy. Mina shot toward the back door and eased it open and shut before Cook noticed.

Outside, brisk evening air slapped her cheeks, and she shivered as she dashed to the back gate of the small courtyard. She yanked it open, and when Will turned toward her at the creak of the hinges, the night lost its chill.

"Good evening, Mina. Though I can't say I like this stealthy business, I am happy you came." He offered his arm. "Shall we?"

"We shall." She smiled. How could she not? The gleam in Will's eyes pulled her into the adventure of the evening, erasing the smudge of Gilbert Grimlock on her day and easing the tension of trying to slip out unnoticed.

Together, they stepped into the evening throng of London's streets. The aged thoroughfares never slept. Gas lamps glowed like miniature suns, lighting their way. They strolled past shift workers going to and from factory jobs, washerwomen scurrying home to feed their families, and even a few children peddling matches or candle stubs.

Down at the next corner, William hailed a cab, twice the size of the one they'd ridden in when they'd gone to tea, with four wheels instead of only two.

She grasped Will's hand and climbed into the carriage. But this time when he shut the door, sealing them in shadowy possibilities, her high spirits faltered. If Father knew what she was about, his wrath would be unbearable. And well deserved. This was scandalous. *She* was scandalous. But was not man's life worth a ruined reputation?

Will sank onto the seat across from her, and she edged into the corner, as far from him as possible. What a sorry tale this might turn out to be were William Barlow not a man of integrity, which he was. Wasn't he? She swallowed. What did she really know of him other than her inflated imaginary image?

"Mina, I..." Spare light crept in as they passed near a streetlamp, highlighting a strange look on his face. He worked his jaw as if he struggled for words. Did he feel the gravity of their charade as much as she?

But then half a smile quirked his lips, and a familiar twinkle reignited in his eyes. "What I mean to say is that I appreciate you coming along for the sake of my uncle. I realize I've put you in somewhat of a compromising situation, and I will strive to protect your reputation. I vow I shall have you home at a decent hour."

So, he did understand. Warmth flared in her chest. Will was gallant after all, a true hero, and she chided herself for having doubted him. "Thank you. And yes, if you don't mind, as soon as your uncle names his heir, I really must return to the inn."

"Understood." He nodded. "Let's hope it's not a fourteen-course meal, hmm?"

Fourteen courses? How long would that take? She sucked in a sharp breath. "Oh! Do you think—?"

"It was only a jest, Mina, and a poor one at that. Forgive me?" A lopsided grin played across his face. "You shall return to your regular life in no time and not be bothered with mine."

She turned her face to the window. His words echoed like a death knell, clanging loud and deep in her soul. Once this night was over, they'd go back to their lives. He stopping by for a pint now and then, and she pressing her nose to the glass each time he left. Endless hours of serving customers and dodging pinches. Helping Martha shell peas or Father manage deliveries. A regular life? How dismal.

But there was no sense dwelling on such melancholy thoughts now, especially when some good may come of this evening, *if* Will were named heir. And if nothing else, she'd have gotten to share a cab with a handsome gentleman and attend a fancy dinner, just like in one of her novels. As the wheels of the carriage bumped over cobblestones, she straightened in her seat and determined to enjoy the ride, no matter what the next hours might bring.

The cab halted, and when her feet touched ground, she stared up at a magnificent, three-story building. It was hard to tell if the bricks were brown or deep red in the darkness, but regardless, the proud structure stood like a soldier on parade. Candles burned in every window, and merry gas lamps flickered on each side of a grand front door. It was a jolly sight. Like a new friend bright eyed at the prospect of meeting her. She followed Will up the stairs and onto the landing, where he rapped a lion-headed knocker against the door.

Moments later, golden light poured out the opening, draping a luminous mantle on the shoulders of a butler in a black suit. He bowed his head and swept out his arm in invitation. "Good evening, Mr. Barlow. If you and your lady would step this way."

Leaving behind the chill November night, Mina stepped into a June morning—or so it seemed. Brilliant light bathed the large foyer, and long-fronded ferns and other plants sat on pedestals of varying heights around the perimeter. How magical! She might almost imagine herself at the center of an enchanted garden.

Will helped her from her coat and handed it over to another servant, then doffed his as well. The butler led them to a sitting room, where Uncle Barlow rose from his seat the moment she met his gaze. Beside him, perched on the edge of a settee, Percy and Alice pouted, or maybe frowned. It was hard to tell. A surprising twinge of pity squeezed Mina's heart. How awful to go through life with a perpetual sourness festering inside.

Uncle Barlow clapped William on the back with a "Happy you made it, my boy." Then he stopped in front of her. His big hand gathered her fingers, and he pressed a light kiss atop them. " 'The pain of parting is nothing to the joy of meeting again.' "

She grinned at his Dickens quote. How sweet that he'd remembered her love for *Nicholas Nickleby*. "Thank you, sir, but the pleasure is mine."

He released her and chuckled. "I didn't think it possible, William, but your wife's charm outshines yours."

Will's gaze sought hers, and a strange gleam deepened the blue in his eyes—a look she'd never before seen from him.

Will cleared his throat and, in a flash, the look disappeared, replaced by a familiar playful twinkle. "She is rather brilliant, is she not?"

Across the room, Percy rose like a black cloud of doom, pulling Alice up along with him. "We are here for dinner, I believe. And I, for one, am famished, Uncle."

"Well then." Uncle Barlow rubbed his hands together. "I suppose we shall have to remedy that, eh?"

He led their entourage out of the sitting room and into a corridor lined with oil paintings and crystal wall sconces. Mina soaked it all in as she walked at Will's side, memorizing the way light played off the gilded frames and the softness of the thick Persian runner beneath her feet. She blinked, praying the dream would not fade. This was a storybook palace, and she was a princess strolling next to her prince.

"Look at that gown." Behind her, Alice's ugly whisper stabbed her in the back. "Puffed sleeves went out of fashion at least three seasons ago. And not a glimmer of jewels, not even some simple earbobs."

"Knowing my cousin," Percy rumbled in a low voice, "it's the best they can afford. Elizabeth Hill did right when she cut him loose, for he's likely neck-deep in debt. Obviously this woman was too dull witted to credit his faults and pull out before it was too late."

"I'd say she is a drab."

The venom in their remarks worked a slow burn up her neck, dimming some of the grandeur of Uncle Barlow's fine home. . .and who was Elizabeth Hill?

Will leaned close, his breath warm against her ear, making her forget about his cousins' jabs and a woman named Elizabeth—especially when he whispered for her alone, "Ignore them, Mina. You look lovely and would even had you worn your taproom apron."

Oh, dear. Now heat flooded beyond her neck and spread in a

flame across her cheeks. She dipped her head as they entered the dining room, lest he see the effect.

Uncle Barlow stopped in front of a large table draped with white linen and sporting silver-edged place settings. "I've taken the liberty to arrange seating. Percy and Mina on this side." He lifted his right hand. "Alice and William, opposite, if you please."

Percy skirted past her to grab the chair nearest Uncle Barlow's, then backed off at the grim shake of Uncle's head. Uncle Barlow advanced and held the chair out for Mina. Across from her, William did the same for Alice.

As soon as all were seated, servants entered, placing domed platters atop the table. When they lifted the lids, Alice and Percy leaned forward, eyes narrowed at the food.

Mina settled her napkin in her lap. Whatever Will's cousins were concerned about now, at least they weren't scrutinizing her, and she could go back to reveling in her fairy-tale night. Uncle Barlow slid a browned piece of roasted fowl from a serving platter onto her plate, then spooned an accompanying gravy atop it. The savory scent rained drops at the back of her throat. If she could remember everything about this dish, perhaps Martha might be able to copy it.

Across from her, Alice sniffed and stared at Uncle Barlow. "Is something the matter with your cook?"

"No, nothing at all." Uncle speared a large bite of his meat and chewed with such gusto, the tufts of hair near his ears jittered. "Why do you ask?"

"No soup? No fish course? We begin with naught but a main dish?"

"Do you object to fowl?"

Alice's lips puckered for a moment. "No."

"Then why not enjoy what has been served?" Uncle Barlow chuckled. "I assure you, it is by no mistake I have chosen to reduce the courses. A year ago now, my physician suggested my gout might improve should I lose a stone or two. It has, and so I continue to eat a lighter fare."

A rumble sounded deep in his chest, and he pulled out his handkerchief. His cough wasn't as hacking this time though, and for his sake, Mina hoped he was truly on the mend.

"Humph," Alice grumbled, then looked down her nose at Mina. "I suppose this is a feast for you."

She smiled, ignoring that somehow Alice meant her words as a cut. But how could they be? This *was* a feast, for she'd never sampled anything like it. The rich aftertaste of her first bite yet lingered in her mouth. "It is quite delicious."

"I agree." Across the table, William winked at her.

From the corner of her eye, she noted that Percy didn't eat his meal. Odd, for was he not the one who'd declared himself famished? He pulled out a slip of paper and a pencil from his pocket then scribbled down some sort of note, all beneath the cover of the table. The others couldn't see, but she did. Why would he be writing instead of eating?

"Mina." Uncle Barlow tapped a finger on the table, drawing her attention. "Do you remember the scenes in *Bleak House* when old Smallweed demands Judy to 'shake him up'?"

"I do." She set down her fork, a grin spreading. "I own that we are supposed to loathe the man, but secretly"—she inclined her face toward Will's uncle and lowered her voice—"I rather liked him."

"Ha ha! So did I." Uncle Barlow raised a fist in the air and gruffed out in his best Smallweed imitation, " 'Shake me up, Judy. You brimstone beast!' "

Mina laughed, not just from the man's antics, but also from the raised brows on both Will and Alice.

Percy turned slightly away from them all, scribbling furiously. Mina's laughter faded. Whatever Percy was taking notes on couldn't be good, not if he must hide the contents.

"Tell me, William," Uncle Barlow's voice rumbled. "Has your

wife made a reader of you yet?"

Her face shot to Will's. The reminder that Uncle Barlow thought them married was an unpleasant jolt, and worse, that it was their deception alone that had earned her a seat at his table.

The tips of Will's ears reddened. "Not yet, sir."

"Well I"—Alice interrupted—"find reading tiresome. Tell me, Mina." She dabbed her lips with a napkin, as if speaking her name was a stain to be rubbed off. "Do you not find it hard to distinguish fact from reality after immersing yourself in falsehoods? For that is what novels are, are they not? A great collection of fabrications and imaginary people?"

Falsehoods! She ground her teeth so hard, her jaw crackled. Even if she had thought to bring along Effie's second-chance coin, the anger simmering in her belly would've made it impossible to extend Alice such a charity.

Uncle Barlow leaned sideways and patted Mina's arm. "Pay her no mind, my dear. I should much rather live in a world of unicorns and fairies."

Next to Mina, Percy's small pencil flew with a life of its own. She opened her mouth to call him out, but then servants descended, removing their plates and setting before each of them a steamed pudding decorated with laurel leaves. Clove and cinnamon wafted up in a heavenly cloud, and she couldn't help but bend and inhale a great, spicy breath. Ignoring Percy, she took a bite. Sweet apples in a thick sauce had been baked within sponge cake, all soaked in some kind of mulled liqueur and lightened with dollops of cream. Absolute perfection filled her mouth. Martha would never be able to recreate this.

Uncle Barlow shoved his dish away after only a few bites. For a moment, Mina held her spoon in midair. Was it proper etiquette to continue eating if the host had clearly finished?

But across from her, Will's spoon dipped into his pudding, and he took another big bite, paying no mind whatsoever to his uncle's obviously sated appetite. She'd have to ask him about it later—on the ride home, perhaps—because for now, she determined to finish every last bit of her dessert.

Percy's pencil flew from his hand, landing on the carpet next to his chair. He shoved his paper back into his pocket then bent to retrieve the pencil, but in his haste, hadn't tucked the note in deep enough. The small slip of paper fluttered out and landed near the edge of the chair, teetering on the cushion. Any minute and it would plummet to the floor.

Without thinking, Mina snatched the thing, curious as to what he'd been documenting; but as the paper came away in her fingers, guilt churned the sweets in her stomach. Was she now a thief as well as a deceiver? What had gotten into her?

She reached to return the slip, but just then Percy straightened. Any further movement on her part, and she'd be caught red-handed.

She froze. What was she to do now?

CHAPTER ELEVEN

What lawsuits grow out of the graves of rich men, every day;
sowing perjury, hatred, and lies among near kindred,
where there should be nothing but love!
Martin Chuzzlewit

Will studied Mina across the table—as he had been doing all
night when she wasn't looking. Fine, white teeth worried her
lower lip, and an endearing little crinkle weighted her brow. What
on earth was she puzzling over?

He looked closer. In the past year as he'd frequented the Golden
Egg, why had he never noticed the sweet, tiny freckles sprinkled
over the top of her nose? Or the flaming streaks of copper in her
hair? When had she grown into such a beauty?

"Now that dinner is finished," Uncle Barlow said while folding
his napkin. "I suppose we should be about our business, eh?"

"Finally," Alice gruffed out beneath her breath, then in a
louder, more syrupy tone, "Dearest Uncle, should you like Mina
and me to retire to another room so that you men may confer in
private?"

"No need." He held up his hand, staving her off. "It is my
experience that wives are an integral part in how a household is
run, and it is the running of my household that I am most interested in."

"Even so, Uncle Barlow, if you don't mind, I must plead a
moment for myself." Mina pushed back her chair and shot to her
feet. "Will you excuse me?"

Will cocked his head. Why the sudden need to escape?

"Of course, my dear. The necessary room is the third door on the left." Uncle stood.

So did Will.

But Percy was too busy fumbling with something in his pocket to pay Mina any such respect. Or did the scoundrel feign the preoccupation just to snub her? Oh, how he'd love to reach across the table and yank his cousin from his chair, but he forced his feet to remain still. Schoolboy theatrics probably didn't fit the type of behaviour Uncle was looking for in an heir. Swallowing his disgust, he lowered to his seat as Mina disappeared out the door.

Uncle Barlow planted his elbows on the table and steepled his fingers, tapping them together. "I have one simple question for each of you." His gaze swung to Percy. "I shall ask you first, Percival, being you are the eldest by several months. Should you be named heir, what do you intend to do with the estate once I am gone?"

A shrill titter squealed out of Alice, like that of a rabbit being stepped upon. "Oh! My husband is brilliant when it comes to finance. Wait until you hear his plans. He's going to—"

"I believe I asked my nephew." Uncle curbed her with a glare from beneath his shaggy brows. "If you don't mind?"

Her mouth puckered into a clam ripple. "No, of course not."

Will coughed into his hand, stifling a grin. Between Alice and Mina, there was no contest as to where Uncle's affections lay, and increasingly, his. Bless Mina's heart. She was a sunbeam to Alice's heavy, dark cloud.

Percy straightened in his seat, resettling his glasses just so on the bridge of his nose. After a quick smoothing of any wrinkles on each coat sleeve, he faced Uncle Barlow as if addressing the prime minister.

"The fact of the matter is that my wife is correct." Percy tilted his head in a superior manner. Gads! If he lifted his nose any higher, a nosebleed might follow.

"You see, Uncle Barlow, there are not many men more well-versed in finance than I. That being said, I believe that the future lies in rails. With the innovation of the steam engine, and the largest station in all of Europe recently opened right here in London, it's obvious that railroad investment is the way to go."

Uncle Barlow grunted. "Perhaps."

Will folded his arms and leaned back in his chair. Judging by the rise of Percy's chest, the man was about to launch into one of his unending soliloquies.

"There is no perhaps about it." Reaching inside his suit coat, Percy pulled out a sheaf of papers.

Will gaped. How had the man concealed such a thick wad of documents?

"I have taken the liberty of running up the numbers. If you'll just look here." Shoving aside the dishes, Percy spread the papers onto the table and stabbed one in particular with his index finger. "This graph shows that railroads are soon to be the lifeblood of commerce. According to a recent tabulation comparing canals to roads to rails, the upswing is soon to be steam engines. In fact, out of pocket expenses pale in comparison to. . ."

His cousin droned on, but Will was more interested in what his uncle might think of the presentation. Was he wearied with Percy's statistics or eager to find out more? He slipped a covert glance at the old fellow, but his uncle's grey eyes neither drooped with boredom nor shone with interest. Only once did Uncle reach for his handkerchief to accommodate a short coughing spell.

Beyond Uncle Barlow, a shadow appeared on the threshold. Will leaned back farther in his chair for a better look. Mina hovered like a spectre, neither entering nor retreating. She lingered, her eyes wide and beseeching his. In ghostlike fashion, she crooked her finger and beckoned him. What the deuce?

"—William?"

He jerked his gaze back to Uncle Barlow, who stared at him in expectation.

"S–Sorry?" he stammered.

"I said I've gathered enough information from your cousin. It is your turn, my boy, to make clear your position. What are your intentions should you inherit my estate?"

In the doorway, Mina swept her entire hand toward the corridor, pulling his attention once more back to her. Clearly, she signaled him to join her, but why now? Did she not realize—

"Well William?"

He jerked his face back to Uncle. "Nothing," he answered.

Alice and Percy gasped in unison.

"Nothing?" Uncle Barlow repeated.

Behind his uncle, Mina upped her frantic gesturing.

Sweet heavens! What was he to do? Whatever Mina had to say was clearly urgent, but this was his chance—perhaps his only one—to persuade Uncle and thwart Percy's wicked scheme. He straightened his shoulders. Mina would have to wait. "What I mean to say is that I intend to move into your country estate and run things as you always have. Your tenants rely upon the land for their livelihood, and I can't see putting them out of their homes." He narrowed his eyes at Percy. "Not even for the sake of investment."

Red crept up his cousin's neck. "If the master prospers, so do the servants."

"Yet if the master is ruined, so are the tenants," he shot back.

"If one does not risk"—Alice's shrewish voice cut in—"one does not gain."

He frowned at her. "But gains are not always positive. Unwarranted risk often reaps ills such as sorrow, debt, prison, or worse."

"Which you know firsthand." Percy leveled the words at him like a loaded rifle. "But I wonder, Cousin, if you have learned your gambling lessons, or would you even now wile away Uncle's money at a gaming table without a second thought?"

Uncle Barlow shifted in his chair, and Will clenched his jaw. Blast his cousin for reminding the old man of his ignoble past.

Mina yet bobbed in the doorway, but he couldn't very well join her now and leave Percy to fill Uncle's head with more reminders of his questionable history. If Uncle Barlow based his decision on the exploits of his younger years, he'd never be named heir. But how could he prove he wasn't that man anymore and that his pompous cousin didn't deserve to—Pompous? That may be the key. Were he to humble himself, perhaps Uncle Barlow might extend some grace, for the man did have a merciful side to him.

Disregarding the sneer twisting Percy's lips, Will turned to Uncle. "Percy is right. As you well know, I have experienced the degradation caused by my own poor choices. I offer you no excuse whatsoever for my reckless past and am, in fact, shamed by it. Yet I am not the man I once was, thanks to you—and God—for giving me a second chance when I was at my lowest point. I assure you, Uncle, that I have mended my ways. Whether or not you choose to believe such, I leave in your hands, for I trust you to make a sound decision."

A smile curved Uncle's mouth, crinkling his skin well up to the corners of his eyes. "Well said, my boy. Well said."

Alice reared back her head, barely disguising her breathed out "Pish!"

Percy collected his papers, stacked them in a neat pile, then shoved the whole thing toward Uncle. "Facts over sentiment, I always say. Read for yourself, on this top document right here, you will see—"

"Excuse me. I won't be but a moment." Will pushed back his chair and stood before Percy launched into a lecture on the merits of steam engines. With his cousin so diverted, this would be the best time to safely see to Mina.

He strode out of the dining room, and as soon as he stepped into the corridor, Mina urged him away from the door with a tip of her head. Intrigued, he followed.

"I must speak with you," she whispered. "Alone."

Something dreadful crept in from the edges of her voice, and he reached for her hand. "Very well. Come along." He led her down the passage and pulled her into the sitting room.

"What is it?" He spoke low, her clear desire for secrecy tempering his tone.

"I think I have your proof." She held out an unfolded slip of paper.

Collecting it, he scanned the words.

> *Picks at his food.*
> *Wishes to live with unicorns.*
> *Believes in fairies.*
> *Outbursts claiming brimstone beasts.*

He frowned at the gibberish, then met Mina's gaze. "What is this?"

"Your cousin Percy has been taking notes all evening. Every time your uncle does something questionable, he writes it down. Oh, Will—" Her voice frayed to a ragged thread. "I think he's documenting things out of context to incriminate your uncle, preparing even now to have him committed."

The truth of her words punched him hard, and a growl rumbled in his throat. What a cur! What a wicked, grasping cur. The confirmation of Percy's true intent tightened his gut, and the paper shook in his hand. This had to stop, here and now. He wheeled about and strode to the corridor.

"Will?" Mina's voice trembled behind him—and he hated the fear he'd caused by his abrupt departure. But it couldn't be helped.

He never should have dragged her into this.

"What are you going to do?"

He upped his pace, not daring to give her an answer. What he'd like to do would land him behind bars.

Chapter Twelve

If our affections be tried, our affections are our consolation
and comfort; and memory, however sad, is the best
and purest link between this world and a better.
Nicholas Nickleby

Mina sped after Will. She'd never seen him take such a warrior stance—and a shiver slid across her shoulders. She'd hate to be on the receiving end of the wrath she'd witnessed hardening his jawline.

Will stalked into the dining room and slammed the note down in front of Uncle Barlow, the movement knocking loose a pile of papers she'd not seen before she'd excused herself from the room.

"What do you think you're doing?" Percy scrambled to collect the fluttering pages.

"There is one paper my cousin neglected to show you, Uncle." William jammed his finger at the note. "Read it."

"What are you going on about—" Alice's words crashed to a halt as her gaze landed on the scribbled writing in front of Uncle Barlow. She reached to snatch the incriminating paper away, but Will's uncle beat her to it.

Uncle Barlow's lips moved as he read over the words, then he frowned up at Will. "What is the meaning of this?"

"The meaning, sir, is that my cousins intend to have you committed to an asylum."

Mina held her breath. The sudden silence in the dining room was a living thing. A breathing monster. The kind that writhed and nipped. She huddled closer to Will. Were this a novel, she'd skip to the next chapter to see how things turned out.

Percy shoved his glasses tight against the bridge of his nose, as if battening down the hatches before a great storm. Then he threw back his shoulders and faced Uncle Barlow. "I assure you, Uncle, whatever doubts my cousin is trying to implant in your head can be nothing but a scheme to garner himself the inheritance."

Uncle Barlow grunted. "Did you write this note, Percival?"

"I did."

Mina blinked. How stunning. He admitted to the offense without hesitation?

But even more stunning, Percy slid his narrowed gaze to her. Lamplight flashed off his spectacles like lightning bolts. "The real criminal here is William's wife, for she stole the paper from my pocket."

"Mina?" Uncle Barlow turned in his seat, the questions in his gaze driving her back a step. "Did you pick Percy's pocket?"

"I—I. . .no!" She gasped. How had things gotten so turned around? "I took nothing from his pocket. The paper fell out and was about to plummet to the floor, when I simply caught the thing. I thought to give it back, but I—I—"

"There is no need to defend yourself for retrieving a fallen paper, Mina." Will reached out defiantly and entwined his fingers with hers. "The only crime here is Percy's clear indictment of you, Uncle."

"Indictment? Flit!" Percy swatted his hand in the air as if slapping away an annoying black fly. "Such skulduggery can only be imagined in the mind of a deviant. I was merely keeping notes of this momentous evening for posterity's sake."

A snort ripped out of Will. "You seriously expect us to believe that?"

"I should think my word is of more value than that of some law clerk wastrel and his no-account bride. Her ill breeding was apparent even before she resorted to thievery. She suits you though. Far better than Elizabeth ever did. Two unscrupulous peas in a pod, I'd say."

"Enough!" Uncle Barlow roared and all eyes swung his way. He stood and slapped both palms on the table. "I can see my decision will require more effort than I first anticipated, as you've all given me quite a lot to think about. In light of such, we shall reconvene at my country estate over Christmas. Arrive the week before. Until then, I bid you good night."

Uncle Barlow strode from the room, leaving them agape with the sudden departure. So many questions tumbled about in Mina's mind, that she was glad for Will's strong hold of her hand, grounding her. Of course she couldn't possibly go to Uncle Barlow's country estate. How would Will explain that? And who was this Elizabeth that kept getting mentioned?

Percy jumped to his feet, his chair teetering on two legs. He stalked toward Will and speared his chest with a pudgy finger. "This isn't finished, Cousin." He emphasized each word with a jab.

"No, it is not." Will spun, his grip on her hand pulling her with him. "Come along, Mina."

Her feet double-timed to keep up with his long stride, though she couldn't blame him. She wished to leave Percy and Alice behind every bit as much as he. In the foyer, a servant waited with their wraps, and Will helped her into her coat before he donned his. By the time Alice's and Percy's footsteps clipped onto the marble floor, Will led her out the front door.

At the bottom of the stairs, he turned to her. "Mind if we walk a bit before I hail a cab?"

She glanced back at the townhouse. No sign of his cousins yet, but they were sure to appear soon. "Well, I don't fancy waiting here."

He didn't say anything, but the approval in his eyes warmed her in the brisk evening air. They didn't stroll far before a hansom rolled along and Will flagged it down. He opened the door for her and helped her in, then hopped up himself, calling out to the jarvey,

"The Golden Egg Inn on Chicory Lane."

She settled her skirts on the seat as the carriage lurched into motion, springs squeaking and bouncier than normal.

Across from her, Will took off his hat and raked his fingers through his hair. The glow of a streetlamp shone in the window, tracing a grimace on his face. "I am sorry, Mina, about the whole evening. I should not have exposed you to my family in the first place. Percy and Alice had no right to say such ghastly things about you."

Despite the chill of the evening, his defense of her wrapped around her shoulders like a warm embrace. "Well, if nothing else"—a small smile ghosted her lips—"this evening has made me realize that perhaps life at the inn isn't as bad as I imagine it to be. Father is strict, but at least he is not spiteful. Our cook may be outspoken, but her words are kind. And"—her smile grew—"I did get to dine in a London townhouse just like a real lady."

"Oh, Mina, you are a real lady. You are—" His voice cracked along the edges, and he cleared his throat. "You are something special. Very special. I hope you know that."

"Thank you," she murmured, unsure if he could even hear the words for the way her throat closed around them.

Will blew out a disgusted breath. "But blast that Percy for being a scoundrel. To have such blatant evidence brought against him and then turn it around that way. The devil could learn a trick or two from him."

His head hung, and her heart broke. Gone was the carefree man laughing over a mug with his good friend. This William Barlow was a stranger, with his shoulders bowed by the weight of how to rescue his uncle. That he loved the old fellow was more than evident.

Her admiration for him grew, as did her pity. "What will you do now?"

He straightened, yet said nothing more. For a while he looked out the window at the passing streetlights, then eventually heaved a sigh. "I don't know. There's nothing to do but look for more evidence, I suppose. Christmasing at Uncle's estate ought to give me ample time to find something." He turned his face back to her. "Mina, if you are willing, and if I approached your father, do you think he'd give you permission to travel with me?"

"Over Christmas?" The words squeaked out of her. What a dream that would be. Snowflakes and sleigh rides and an estate swagged with greenery. What a story to live inside of! But as the carriage juddered along the cobbles of London's streets, reality smacked her hard. What was she thinking? Father would never let her go. And besides, continuing the charade would only cause more harm than good, for surely they'd be found out. An afternoon tea or an evening dinner was a far cry from spending an entire week together.

She shook her head. "I don't think so. It may be time for you to tell your uncle the truth of us. Surely if you explain we were only trying to save him from the possibility of an asylum, he would understand."

Will grunted. "He would have, had I not ruined my testimony in my younger years." His haunted gaze met hers. "I came up with some fancily embroidered lies in the past in order to gain my uncle's money. I am certain he cannot help but wonder if I have changed. Sometimes I wonder myself."

His mouth twisted as if he sucked on bitter whortleberries; then he sank back against the cushion and rode in silence the rest of the way, apparently lost in thought.

So did she. How did one make someone believe the truth when the truth had been based on a lie? The question played over and over in her head until the cab jerked to a stop. Will helped her out and faced her. Even in the darkness, a strange light gleamed in his eyes, and he stepped closer.

"Mina. . ." Her name on his lips was like a kiss, and he bent closer.

The space between them came alive with promise. Her heart

pulsed in a crazed beat, throbbing in her wrists, jittering her knees. If he leaned, just barely, his mouth would be on hers.

She swallowed. What was she thinking? He was a man of means and possibly a future heir to an estate. She was nothing but a girl who ran mugs of ale and plates of sausages to hungry men. It had been a lovely dream—but one built on a lie. It was time to be done.

"Good night, Will," she blurted, then whirled toward the front door.

Her fingers pressed against the wood, about to thrust the thing open, when she froze. She couldn't very well waltz into the taproom wearing her best coat and gown and not expect to meet a few tawdry remarks. Or worse—run straight into Gilbert Grimlock.

She hesitated, waiting for the cab door to close and horses' hooves to clop off, then darted around to the back. What a ninny. So many things had happened tonight that she hardly knew what to think.

Shoving open the courtyard door, she slowed her breathing, then crossed to the kitchen entrance. She eased the latch handle open, releasing the lock. If God smiled upon her, Martha would either be dozing in her corner chair or absent altogether.

Slowly, she nudged the door open, bit by bit, then slipped inside. A single lamp glowed on the counter. Clean dishes sat atop cupboard shelves, and scattered on the worktable were Christmas pudding moulds of various shapes and sizes—most dented, all tarnished. The sight pulled her brows into a frown. No doubt Uncle Barlow's kitchen contained moulds that shone like an August sun.

Holding her breath, she slipped her glance to the corner—but no Martha. No "peas and porridge" or "peas and anything," for Cook's chair sat empty. Her gaze drifted to the work clock ticking away on the wall. Eleven o'clock? By faith! It was later than she'd accounted.

A slow smile twitched her lips. Why hadn't she thought of that before? Mr. Grimlock was surely abed by now. She needn't have rushed the evening after all.

The tension in her shoulders unwound, and she turned to secure the door. She'd just have to take care when she climbed the stairs and passed by his chambers on her way to her own. The floorboard in front of his door was notoriously squeak—

"Mina?"

She whirled. A gargoyle stood on the threshold, beak nosed and beady eyed, blocking the escape to her room.

Gilbert Grimlock.

CHAPTER THIRTEEN

Moths, and all sorts of ugly creatures. . .
hover about a lighted candle. Can the candle help it?
Great Expectations

Mina clutched her hands in front of her, vainly seeking some kind of support to withstand the malignant gaze of Gilbert Grimlock. Rifling through a hundred excuses she could offer the man, she discarded each one in turn, even while knowing the longer she stood there without saying something, the guiltier she appeared to be.

"I—I thought you to be abed, sir. I. . ." Her words languished. Apparently opening her mouth and expecting some sort of alibi to slip out wasn't the most brilliant of strategies.

Mr. Grimlock stalked from the doorway, advancing toward her. He was a boggy sort of fellow, with his ever-present sheen of perspiration winking on his brow and coating his upper lip. The fabric beneath his arms darkened in circles, lending to his appearance of being perpetually moist. The man was a fungus. A black mold, the kind that if inhaled would settle deep in the lungs and force one to cough out the violation.

He stopped inches in front of her, far too close for propriety, bringing with him the sickening smell of potatoes left too long in a cellar. "There are still a few patrons in the taproom. My duty is the management of this inn during your father's absence. I can't very well do that with my eyes closed." Bending, he studied her, his dark gaze spreading over her skin like a rash. "I thought you suffered from a headache?"

"I do—I mean I did." It took everything in her to keep from fleeing out the back door. Instead, she forced her hands to smooth down her skirts, hating that her palms had acquired the same moistness that Mr. Grimlock embodied. "My headache is much better now. Thank you for inquiring, and I am sorry if I disturbed you. Good night, Mr. Grimlock."

She edged past him.

But he sidestepped, blocking her, and grabbed her shoulders. "Your coat is cold and damp. Where have you been at this time of night?"

"I—" She froze. What to say? She certainly couldn't admit to romping about the London streets in a carriage alone with a man. "I had a previous engagement I could not miss."

Mr. Grimlock's eyes narrowed to thin slits. Small dots of perspiration glimmered on his forehead from the movement. "What kind of engagement could you have possibly had at this time of night?"

"A private one."

"Private?" With the crook of his finger, he lifted her chin. "I wonder what kind that could be?"

She stiffened beneath the touch of his calloused skin, rough and far too heated. "Excuse me, Mr. Grimlock, but it is late, and I should like to retire."

He bent closer, nearly nose to nose, his knuckle drifting down from her chin and tracing a line against the bare skin of her neck.

This was not to be borne! She wrenched away. "How dare you!"

One of his brows arched, and a single, crude drip broke free from the collection of wet dots on his forehead and trickled down his temple. "How dare I? I am not the one roaming the streets at night. Unless you tell me what you've been about, your father shall hear of this."

Fury ignited deep in her belly, shooting up sparks and shaking through her. "I will not be bullied around by you, sir. You can be sure my father will hear of this, for I shall tell him of your untoward behaviour."

She darted sideways.

But his hand shot out, and he grabbed her arm. "Not so fast. You never did answer me, and I will not be put off. Where were you tonight?"

"It is none of your business. Good night, Mr. Grimlock." She jerked aside—and his fingers dug into the tender part of her upper arm, clasping her all the tighter and pulling her to him. Even through the thickness of her coat and gown, the moisture of him seeped into her clothing.

"The business of the inn *is* my business until your father returns." His breath landed hot on her neck, leaving a clammy vapor behind where it touched.

"Let me go! My life is not part of that business."

"It could be, if only you would let it. I have your father's approval. You have but to say the word, and you could be Mrs. Grimlock by Christmas. We will run this inn together someday, you and I."

The thought of marriage to this beast—especially the marriage bed—surged a strong revulsion through her veins, and she yanked from his grip, the force violent enough that they both staggered.

She used the momentum to finally fly past him. "Good night, Mr. Grimlock."

An oily chuckle followed her down the corridor. "See you in the morning, Mina."

She dashed up the stairs and darted into her room, shut and locked the door, then leaned back against it. She'd not be able to hold off Mr. Grimlock for much longer. Closing her eyes, she forced away the awful image of his sweaty visage.

If only Will had asked her to be his real bride.

Chapter Fourteen

Love her, love her, love her! If she favours you, love her.
If she wounds you, love her. If she tears your heart to pieces—
and as it gets older and stronger it will tear
deeper—love her, love her, love her!
Great Expectations

Will stared at the affidavit on his desk. Which barrister had requested this? Bagley? Whimpole? Snavesgate? As hard as he tried to remember, all that came to mind was a sprinkle of freckles on creamy skin, doe-like blue eyes blinking up into his, and a tremulous smile on lips that had been close enough to kiss. When had Mina Scott become such an enigmatic beauty—one he couldn't get out of his head?

"Come on." Fitz's voice pulled his attention away from the stack of documents. His friend shoved his coat and hat toward him, nearly knocking him backward on his stool.

Will grabbed the things out of reflex and glanced at the wall clock, then frowned up at Fitz. "Where are we going? It's only half past two."

"You need some air." Fitz turned on his heel and strode toward the door.

Rising, Will shrugged on his coat and clapped his hat atop his head, trying to make sense of his friend's words. By the time he caught up to Fitz at the top of the stairs, he truly did need some air—and some answers. "What's this all about?"

Fitz paused with his hand on the doorknob. "You just sent that last runner to Harberry Court."

"So?"

"Barrister Grovener's chambers are on the other side of town."

The wind punched out of his lungs. Sweet heavens! That mistake would no doubt come back to sink teeth into him. Fitz was right. A walk in the air might do him some good. He yanked open the other door and beat his friend outside and down the stairs to the sidewalk.

"I can only assume this is about your uncle," Fitz said as soon as he fell into step. "Wasn't that dinner last night? Oh...egad! How callous of me." His friend shot ahead then walked backwards in front of him, concern folding his brow. "You didn't get the inheritance, did you, ol' chap?"

Will shook his head. "Uncle Barlow didn't announce it yet."

"Whew. You had me worried there for a moment." Stepping sideways, Fitz pivoted and once again joined Will's side. "You haven't heard from your mother, have you? Has she fallen into a worse state of health?"

"Not that I know of."

"Well, if it's neither of those things, then what has you so addlepated?"

For a moment, he walked in silence, which was easy enough to do with the clamoring of peddlers and passing vehicles making more than enough noise. Fitz's question rattled around in his skull like a penny being dropped into a tin and given a good shake. What was it that bothered him to such a degree?

He glanced sideways at his friend. "I'm not sure, actually. For some reason, I can't stop thinking about last night. I suppose because it was a perfectly awful evening, thanks to my cousins. You should have seen them, Fitz. They were both in rare form. Percy collected bogus evidence I can only assume he plans to use against Uncle Barlow, then he dredged up my past for all to hear. Worse, both he and Alice said horrid things about Mina, behind her back and to her face. Ahh, but Mina. . ."

His pace slowed, and once again Mina Scott's sweet face crowded out the real world. If he listened hard enough, he could still hear the magic of her laughter as she'd bantered with Uncle Barlow.

A tug on his sleeve yanked him sideways, and he barely avoided stepping into a puddle of sewage and ruining his shoes. "Thanks." He gave his friend a sheepish smile. "Looks like I owe you yet again."

Fitz rolled his eyes. "If I had but a farthing for each time you said that, I'd own a matched set of high-steppers and a shiny new barouche. Now then, what about Miss Scott?"

His smile stretched into a grin. "You should have seen her. A champion and a sport. She put up with Alice's jabs and Percy's slights—which as you know isn't easy to do. And she's completely stolen Uncle Barlow's heart."

"Hmm. . . I'm beginning to wonder if she's stolen your heart as well. I didn't think it possible after the way Elizabeth. . .well, you know—"

Fitz continued speaking, but his friend's voice faded, as did the squawking of a nearby vendor hawking apples. All he heard was the rush of blood whooshing in his ears and the echoing repeat of Fitz's words, *"She's stolen your heart as well. She's stolen your heart as well."*

His step hitched. So did his breath. Were Fitz's careless words correct? Shoving down the thought, he shuddered. He'd never again hand over his heart to a woman only to have it sliced open and bled out. Once had been more than enough.

"—announce?" The expectancy written on the curve of Fitz's brow hinted he'd missed a question.

"Announce what?" he asked.

"Who's to be his heir." His friend looked down his nose at him. "This little walk isn't helping, is it?"

"Don't be ridiculous. Of course it is. Uncle Barlow has invited us all to his estate for Christmas, so I expect he'll announce then."

Fitz's eyes widened. "How on earth did you get Miss Scott to agree to that?"

"I haven't. Not yet, anyway."

"I see. Uh. . . ?" Fitz hitched his thumb sideways, indicating the open door of the Brass Rail Pub.

Will shook his head. A mug of ale would only muddle his already fuzzy thinking.

Fitz frowned but kept on walking. "I suppose even if Miss Scott does agree, her father wouldn't allow it. It's not like you're her beau or. . .well, there's a thought for you, eh?"

"How can you even suggest such a thing? No, I shall simply have to persuade her father, that's all."

Fitz cuffed him on the back. "While your tongue is light and quick, I don't think even you can talk your way into gaining his permission to let her go with you."

Tugging the brim of his hat lower, he looked up at Fitz. "You're right. Maybe I do need to become Mina's beau."

"A pretend beau. . .or a real one?"

Exactly. His chest squeezed. So did his breath. "That, my friend, is a question I shall have to think long and hard on."

CHAPTER FIFTEEN

My dear if you could give me a cup of tea to clear the muddle
of my head I should better understand your affairs.
Mrs. Lirriper's Legacy

Tea was life, comfort, all that embodied warmth and fulfillment...
usually. But this afternoon, Mina stared into her cup, finding
no solace whatsoever. Every creak of a floorboard outside the inn's
sitting room door might be Mr. Grimlock on the prowl. Each foot-
step could be his. Dodging the man all day had stretched her nerves
thin, and she just might snap if he dared to breach her weekly tea
with Miss Whymsy.

"What has you so preoccupied, my dear? Is it your father's
return?"

"Hmm?" She glanced up at her old friend. "I'm sorry, but what
were you saying?"

"You see?" Miss Whymsy smiled, the skin at the edges of her
eyes crinkling into soft folds. "Your mind is elsewhere."

She stifled a sigh. There was no hiding anything from a former
governess proficient at coaxing truth from naughty children. "I own
I am a bit pensive, though it has nothing to do with my father.
Please forgive me?"

Her old friend patted her knee. "There is nothing to forgive,
child. Sometimes life has a way of draping about our shoulders and
pressing us down beneath the weight of it. Is there anything I can
do to lighten your burden?"

Her lips twisted into a wry grin. "I don't suppose you'd want to marry Mr. Grimlock so he'd stop pestering me?"

"I don't think he'd be very interested in an old governess." Miss Whymsy set down her teacup, then picked up a book she'd brought along. "Here, this ought to put you in a better frame of mind."

Mina took the novel and ran her fingers over the red cover with gilt type, thrilled yet confused. Had the older lady forgotten she'd already read this title? "Not that I don't appreciate revisiting Mr. Dickens's *A Christmas Carol*, but I must be honest and tell you I've already read it. Several times, in fact."

"Ahh, but you've not read *this* one." Miss Whymsy reached for the book and opened it to the title page.

"Oh, my." Mina sucked in a breath as she stared at the fine, black penmanship scrolled across the paper. "How ever did you manage to come across a signed edition?"

"It's not mine. It is merely on loan from the director of the institute. Which reminds me. . ." Setting the book on the cushion between them, Miss Whymsy folded her hands and leaned forward. "I was wondering if you might speak with your father when he returns today. The institute is fair to bursting with women in need, and much to my regret, I have seen several turned away for lack of space. I know I've asked you before, but I feel I must inquire once again. Is there any chance your father would open up a room or two to house those who are ailing?"

She shook her head. "I don't think—"

But her friend cut her off with a touch to her knee. "Allow me to explain. It wouldn't be for those who are contagious but for those who are on the mend and not quite ready to go home yet. By relocating those women here, it would open up beds for other women in need."

An ache settled deep in her soul, not only for the thought of the sick women being turned away, but for the way Miss Whymsy's faded blue-green eyes glimmered with hope. How awful it would be if her friend fell ill and had nowhere to go.

But no. She steeled herself. Father would never allow it.

"I am sorry, my friend, but especially at this time of year, what with the annual Christmas Eve party, there will be absolutely no space whatsoever at the inn. I would love to help, truly, but I am afraid housing women here is out of the question."

"Posh, child." Miss Whymsy sank back onto the cushions. "I figured as much, but on the off chance, thought I'd ask. And don't sell yourself short. . .you have helped. The money you donated went toward more bandages and dressings. I suppose we shall just have to increase our time petitioning God. Shall we?"

"Of course."

They bowed their heads—but a rap on the door jerked them back up. Mina's heart pounded off rhythm. Had Mr. Grimlock come to further torment her? But surely he wouldn't have knocked. Nor would Father have employed such a courtesy if he had returned.

"Oughtn't you answer that, my dear?"

Miss Whymsy's voice prodded her into action. She stood and crossed to the door.

"Just the person I was looking for." William Barlow, hat in hand, entered, looking far too handsome in his royal blue cutaway suit coat and buff-coloured trousers. His smile warmed her, as did his gaze. "Good afternoon, Mina."

Across the room, Miss Whymsy cleared her throat.

Mina bit her lip. Had the older lady heard the way he'd spoken her Christian name?

Will turned toward Miss Whymsy. "My apologies, madam. I did not realize Miss Scott entertained company." He dipped his head in respect. "William Barlow, at your service."

"Miss Whymsy." Mina swept her hand toward Will. "Allow me to introduce Mr. Barlow. Mr. Barlow, my friend, Miss Whymsy."

"The pleasure is mine, madam. I am sorry to have interrupted. I promise this shan't take long." His gaze swung back to Mina. "But if you don't mind, might I have a quick word with you and your father?"

Her eyes widened. "My father?"

"Yes."

"I—I..." Her words stalled. What in all of God's great goodness could Will possibly have to say to her father? "But he is not—"

"Go on, child." Miss Whymsy interrupted. "Tend to your young man. I shall wait here, for I have a friend to keep me company until you return." She reached for the book.

Will crossed to the door and held it wide. "Shall we then?"

Curious, confused, but mostly nervous Mr. Grimlock might see them, she led Will down the corridor to a small alcove at the end. The space was occupied by a single chair and an end table. A window graced the nook with perfect reading light, and it was a favorite haunt of hers when the weather turned too inclement to be outside.

Will stepped next to her, and she peered up at him, but oh how hard it was to think, let alone speak, when he stood so near. She edged back a bit, until her skirt brushed against the chair. "Why do you wish to see my father?"

He fidgeted with his hat, his fingers playing with the brim. Was he nervous too? "You can't very well spend Christmas at my uncle's estate without your father noticing your absence. So I thought I'd have a word with him."

She shook her head. "As much as I'd like to help with keeping your uncle out of an asylum, there is no chance my father will allow me to go."

"Then I will persuade him, that is unless..." He set his hat on the small table, then straightened. Gathering her hands in his, he looked deep into her eyes.

Her breath caught in her throat. This was a moment she'd read about in stories. Dreamed about at night. Was this real? The heat of his body standing so near sure seemed it, as did the touch of his fingers against hers.

"Mina, I need to know. Do you want to spend Christmas with

me? If you don't, say so, and I shall walk away and not trouble you further."

Trouble? She gaped. Did William Barlow not know the effect he had on her? Could he not feel the trembling in her hands? She did want to be with him, Christmas or any other time of year—but without the lie that both bound and kept them apart.

Swallowing back emotion, she steeled herself for what she must say. "There is nothing I'd like better in all the world, but I cannot—"

"That's all I needed to hear." A brilliant smile deepened his dimples, and he squeezed her hands, pulling her close, wrapping her in his excitement. "Now then, where is your father?"

"He's not yet—"

"Unhand that woman!"

Will turned. She shrank.

"Excuse me." Will's voice hardened, belying the apology in his words. "But the lady and I are having a private conversation, and I will thank you to leave us to it."

Afternoon light highlighted the glisten on Gilbert Grimlock's brow as he scowled at Will. "Who do you think you are, ordering me about?"

Will advanced a step, his jaw clenched. "Not that it signifies to you, but I am Mina's beau."

Her—*what?* She sucked in a breath.

So did Mr. Grimlock. "We'll just see about that," he spit out, then his gaze slid to hers. "Mina, your father has returned."

CHAPTER SIXTEEN

Why, on this day, the great battle was fought on this ground.
The Battle of Life

Will stared at the man stomping away down the corridor. Judging by the pound of his steps, if the fellow had been clutching a gun, Will would be bleeding out on the floor right now. Why such animosity? And why had he allowed that animosity to goad him into such a defense? Declaring to be Mina's beau. Of all things. Not that he hadn't intended to speak to her father about the possibility, but what would this unfavorable start lead to? He'd gone about things the right way with Elizabeth, and that had ended horribly. But this? There was nothing even remotely right about the muddle he'd made of things with Mina.

He turned to where she stood deathly still, her fingers pressed against her mouth.

"Mina?" Closing the distance between them, he gently lowered her hand. Her skin was cold to the touch. "Who was that man?"

Cavernous eyes sought his. "Mr. Grimlock. He manages the inn when my father travels. And if Father has returned—oh, Will!" A little cry caught in her throat. "I am afraid of what kinds of fabrications he'll tell Father."

A surge of protectiveness tightened his gut, and he wrapped his fingers around hers. "Then we must reach your father before he does. Lead the way."

She needed no more encouragement. His legs stretched to keep up with her furious pace. She led him along one passageway, cut through a storage closet with two facing doors, then scurried down a short flight of stairs and turned left, stopping breathless in front of a door—

Where the striped coattails of Mr. Grimlock disappeared.

"I think it best if I go in first." He squeezed her hand then released his hold. "Wait here."

"But—"

"Mina." He pressed his finger to her lips. "All will be well. I vow I shall make things right. Will you trust me in this?"

Her blue gaze held on to his, and slowly, she nodded. The fear, the hope, the shimmer of tears all did strange things to his heart.

"Good girl." He wheeled about. Now, if only he believed his own brave words.

Lord, though I don't deserve it. . . For a moment, his silent prayer faltered along with his step as the truth of his words slapped him. Of course he didn't deserve the ear of God or His help. The Creator of all shouldn't even listen to him after not only being involved in such a great deception but dragging Mina into it as well.

Yet was God not the author of mercy? Of grace? Of second chances?

"Will you trust Me in this?"

The same question he'd asked Mina circled back and punched him in the gut. Either he believed all he'd heard and read of God, or he didn't. He wasn't merely standing in front of an innkeeper's office door, but at a crossroads. One that would make or break his faith.

He sucked in a breath, and blew out another prayer. "I need Your help, Lord. Make me the man Mina expects me to be—and the man You want me to be. I *will* trust You in this."

He strode into the small room, prepared for battle.

Ahead, Mina's father stood behind a paper-strewn desk, shrugging out of a great, woolen travel cloak. Dried mud caked the hem, and as he hung the garment on a peg, clods of grey dirt fell to the floor.

"This man! This is the very man of which I speak." To Will's left, Mr. Grimlock swung out his arm, aiming his index finger like a javelin. "Not two minutes ago did I catch this man trifling with your daughter. The shame of it! The gall, right here beneath your own roof, sir."

Mr. Scott continued to unwind a long muffler from about his neck, placing the wrapper on the same hook as his coat, and then finally, he turned. When his gaze met Will's, his hazel eyes widened, his brows shooting toward his shock of reddish hair—the same colour as Mina's, albeit shorn and faded to rust. "Mr. Barlow? Can it be you?"

Planting his feet, he nodded. "It is me, sir, the very same faithful patron who's frequented your establishment this past year."

"He's a son of Venus. A rake!" Rage purpled Mr. Grimlock's cheeks, spreading up to his ears. "I insist you cast this villain out immediately for the sake of your daughter's virtue."

Mr. Scott's chest expanded as he looked from Grimlock to him. "Well, Mr. Barlow, what have ye to say?"

"Your daughter's virtue is of my utmost concern—which is why I came here to speak with you today." He paused, heart pounding. Crossroads were notorious for danger, especially this one, for he knew it well. Could he really go through with this again?

How could he not?

Perspiration beaded on his brow, and he had no doubt he looked as moist and quivery as the angry man next to him. Even so, he squared his shoulders and looked Mr. Scott straight in the eyes. "I ask your permission, Mr. Scott, to court your daughter."

Mina's father grabbed hold of the back of his desk chair with both hands. "I can hardly believe it," he murmured.

"Mr. Scott!" Mr. Grimlock ducked his head like a bull about to charge. "I insist on my right of first claim to your daughter's hand. We have a verbal agreement, do we not, sir?"

Will stiffened. Why had Mina never mentioned such a thing?

Unless, perhaps, she didn't know? He slid his gaze from Grimlock to Mina's father, thinking on all the times the man had not quite filled his or Fitz's mugs to the brim though they'd paid for fulls. Or the times the ale had tasted distinctly watered down. Mr. Scott was a shrewd businessman—but would he have cut such a deal with the boorish Mr. Grimlock?

"Well. . ." Mr. Scott blew out a long breath, his cheeks puffing, then lifted his face to Mr. Grimlock's. "I did say if Mina didn't take a fancy to any gent before the end of this year, the girl would be yours."

Will's hands curled into fists. Not that fathers didn't frequently arrange marriages, but from the little he knew of Mr. Grimlock, the man was unsuitable for Mina in every way. Still. . .he might be able to use Mr. Scott's unsavory proposition to his advantage. He dared a step closer to the desk. "It is not yet the end of the year, sir. There are four weeks remaining, and Mina's taken a fancy to me."

Her father shook his head, and it was hard to say which creased his brow more—the fatigue of travel or perplexity. "I never saw it coming," he mumbled.

"Don't be absurd." Mr. Grimlock threw out his arms. "Mina can have no idea who is the better man for her. And clearly I am. What does this toff know of running an inn?"

"It is not the inn I intend to pursue."

"You see?" Mr. Grimlock faced Mina's father, thumping his chest with his thumb. "I *am* the superior choice."

Of all the pretention. Percy might be able to learn a trick or two from this arrogant fellow.

Mr. Scott fell silent. Releasing his hold of the chair, he crossed his arms and stroked his chin, clearly deep in thought. That didn't bode well. Mina's father couldn't seriously be considering the arrogant Mr. Grimlock as her future husband. . .could he?

Will strode forward, a righteous indignation burning in his gut, and planted his hands on Mr. Scott's desk. "Ought not your daughter have a say in this? It is her life, after all, that we are bandying about as if she had no stake in the matter."

"Hmm." Mr. Scott gruffed out. "Perhaps ye're right."

"Absurd!" Mr. Grimlock raked his fingers through his hair, standing it on end.

Ignoring the outburst, Mina's father lifted his chin and bellowed, "Mina? Come in here, girl. I know ye're out there!"

Will edged back from the desk, chest tight and breath stuck in his throat. Mina likely wouldn't choose Mr. Grimlock, but what if she didn't choose him either?

Or worse, what if she did? Elizabeth had at one point too—and he still bore the puckered scars on his heart.

CHAPTER SEVENTEEN

That was a memorable day to me, for it made great changes in me.
But it is the same with any life. Imagine one selected day struck
out of it, and think how different its course would have been.
Pause you who read this, and think for a moment of the
long chain of iron or gold, of thorns or flowers,
that would never have bound you, but for the
formation of the first link on one memorable day.
Great Expectations

M ina? Come in here, girl. I know ye're out there!"
Mina clutched great bunches of her skirt as Father's voice
boomed out his office door. Fatigue harshened his words. The tim-
ing of this conversation couldn't have been worse, for her father was
ever ill tempered after having suffered the inconveniences of travel.
What would he say? What had been said? The milk she'd taken in
her tea with Miss Whymsy soured in her stomach. Reading about
such intrigues was far different from living it—and she wasn't sure
she liked it. At all.

Leaving behind the safety of the narrow corridor, she stepped
into the lion's den. Mr. Grimlock turned toward her, looking as if
he might pounce at any moment. His hair stood on end in patches
where he'd tugged it.

Father paced behind his desk, hands clasped at his back. His
clothes were wrinkled, and he had yet to remove his hat.

And Will, God bless him... Will stood tall and proud, an island
of strength in this sea of tension. He stepped aside, making enough

room for her wide skirt, the reassurance in his blue gaze lending her support.

"Mina." Father halted his pacing and faced her. "It's come to this. Ye know I would see ye married, child. Ye must choose between these two suitors. Will you have Mr. Barlow or Mr. Grimlock?"

She pressed her lips tight to keep her jaw from dropping. Of course there was no contest, for Will had ever been her hero since the first day he'd sauntered into the Golden Egg. Was her dream really about to come true?

"This is preposterous!" A fine spray of spittle flew out along with Mr. Grimlock's objection. "You hardly know the man."

"Mr. Grimlock, if ye please." Father skewered the fellow with a scowl. "Mr. Barlow has been a regular patron this past year, is a law clerk of good standing, and I'd wager makes the same amount to care for Mina as you. Am I right, sir?"

"Yes, sir." William nodded. "And there's the distinct possibility I am in line to inherit an estate."

"What a load of tosh." Mr. Grimlock turned to her, the movement wafting a sour odor of mouldered oranges. The stains beneath his arms spread in ever-darkening circles, especially when he threw up his hands. "That young swell could be saying anything to fill your head with fanciful thoughts. I offer you stability. The good Grimlock name. A life of pattern, predictability, and solid parameters. Don't be a fool."

Her hands curled into fists. He knew nothing of Will and even less of her to think she desired to spend the rest of her days in such a lackluster fashion. "Mr. Grimlock," she said through gritted teeth. "I thank you for your offer, yet I choose Mr. Barlow."

She shot her gaze to her father, unwilling to see one more dot of sweat pop out on Mr. Grimlock's forehead. "There, Father, you have my decision."

"No! Impossible." Mr. Grimlock stamped his foot like a petulant tot. "My offer is rescinded. I will have nothing more to do with this inn or you people."

Before anyone could say anything further, Mr. Grimlock whirled and stalked out the door, leaving behind nothing but his ringing voice and a blackened scuff on the wooden floor where his shoe had left a mark.

"Well," Father murmured. "I didn't expect to return home to this."

Mina stiffened. Was he cross that she'd ruined his chances of expanding the inn with Mr. Grimlock as his manager?

Almost imperceptibly at first, a slow smile lifted her father's lips, growing in size until it squinted his eyes a bit. "But. . .I couldn't be happier."

She let out a breath, and her shoulders sagged with the relief of it all.

"Nor could I, sir." William grinned down at her, the gleam in his eyes so pure and brilliant, her knees weakened.

Still. . .she bit her lip. Something wasn't right. While everything in her yearned for this to be real, for William Barlow to be her beau, did he *truly* yearn to be hers? Or was he courting her merely to save his uncle? A good reason, noble and compassionate, but one that left her feeling a bit melancholy. Like a child who received a gift-wrapped box, the exact shape and size of a longed for treasure, yet after untying the ribbons and peeling back the paper, finding the box to be empty.

"Sir." William stepped forward. "I know this is all still new to you, but I request to bring your daughter to my uncle's estate for Christmas."

"Meeting the family, eh?" Father scratched his jaw, his fingers rasping on the whiskers sprouted during his travels. "But not yet. Christmas is a moneymaker for the Golden Egg. I cannot possibly spare the time to play chaperone with you two when there'll be patrons aplenty for me to see to. No, no. . .after the holidays is best."

She exchanged a worried glance with Will. After Christmas

would be too late. But if father couldn't travel with her, then who? She'd need someone discreet. Someone available. Someone...

She clenched her hands to keep from snapping her fingers. "What about Miss Whymsy? The old dear has no one besides us to make merry with during the holiday. Could she not travel with me, if she is agreeable?"

For a moment, her father said nothing, just narrowed his eyes as if studying her suggestion beneath a magnifying glass. "Aye," he drawled. "If she is agreeable."

Finally he doffed his hat and hung it on a peg, then turned and faced Will. "But ye'll have my daughter back here for the Christmas Eve party. It's tradition, and I will not be moved on it."

Will nodded. "I shall have her returned for your famous oyster stew, sir."

She peeked at Will. He'd made the promise with such ease, but how on earth would he keep it?

"Very well. Off with the two o' ye then." Her father swept his hand toward the door. "I've a handsome amount of paperwork to tend to before dinner. Between the three of us," Father lowered his voice and tucked his chin. "Mr. Grimlock weren't all that skilled at innkeeping."

She couldn't help but grin.

"Thank you, sir." William bowed his head.

"Don't be thanking me. Mina's the one that chose ye." He hitched his thumb at her over his shoulder as he strode back to his desk.

Stunned at the whole turn of the afternoon, Mina padded out of the office and into the corridor, Will on her heels.

"He's right, you know."

Will's voice turned her around, and she lifted one brow. "About?"

"I ought to be thanking you, and I do." The dimples on his cheeks deepened as his grin grew. "This may turn out to be the best Christmas ever."

She smiled at his enthusiasm. Indeed, it could be the best Christmas ever—*if* Will truly cared for her. But her smile waned as she searched his face. Did he really want to court her? Or was this all just a ruse?

Tired of half-truths and outright deception, her smile faded altogether. A heroine wouldn't waste away with such doubts but would take a bold stand. She swallowed. Could she be a heroine? Did she even have it in her?

Only one way to find out.

She lifted her chin. "While I hope for your sake, and your uncle's, that this Christmas will turn out for the best, I feel that cannot happen without the truth being spoken. I insist you tell your uncle that we are not married, yet are moving toward such, as soon as possible after we arrive. I cannot stay beneath his roof under such pretense, and in fact, I will not."

She clamped her mouth shut. My, but that had been a bold thing to say. Truly heroic. But what would Will think of her outburst? Would he turn around and march back into Father's office, rescinding his offer as thoroughly as had Mr. Grimlock?

His eyes widened, and for an eternity, he said nothing. Just stared. Eventually, his head dipped an acknowledgement. "You're right of course. I will tell my uncle as soon as I'm able."

"Promise?" she pressed.

"Promise." He bent, and his lips brushed against her forehead.

What he said after that was a mystery. Probably some kind of goodbye, for he strode off and left her standing in the corridor, her knees weak. She lifted her fingertips to her brow, wishing, hoping, *needing* his words to be true.

All of them.

CHAPTER EIGHTEEN

She was truest...in the season of trial,
as all the quietly loyal and good will always be.
A Tale of Two Cities

A re ye sure about this?"
Mina met Effie's gaze in the mirror, purposely avoiding eye contact with the large shears gripped in her friend's hand. Despite Effie's skill with scissors, there would still be patches of shorter hair to have to cover up until it all grew back to the same length. But it was only hair, after all—a trifling thing compared to Mina's other worries. Though she tried not to think on it, she couldn't help but wonder how Will would talk his uncle into allowing them to leave the estate before Christmas. Would it be a long enough visit to expose Percy's wicked intentions? And the question that really niggled...was Will courting her only as a means to an end, or was he truly fond of her?

"Mina?"

"Hmm? Oh, sorry." Shoring herself up by gripping the edge of her chair, she nodded. "Yes, I am certain. Proceed."

"All right then. 'Ere goes."

The scissors snipped, and she shivered.

"Hold still, love. Be bricky for me. Don't want to cut too much."

Long locks of reddish-brown hair landed on the floorboards, and with each one, the world turned more and more watery. *Don't think it. Don't do it.* But despite her mental admonition, the last memory of her mother rose like a spectre, pushing tears overboard and dampening her cheeks. *Oh, mama.* The thin woman in a mouse-coloured gown had sat on the cold flagstones of the asylum floor, arms curled about her knees, rocking and rocking and rocking…the shorn hairs on her head sticking out like pins in a cushion. Had her mother even noticed when her hair had been cut?

Mina sucked in a shaky breath. How different might life have been if Mother hadn't lost the baby, hadn't grieved so hard that both her heart and head had broken?

"There we be. How do ye—Mina?" The shears landed with a clatter on the vanity and Effie lowered to her knees, taking both of Mina's hands in her own. "Are ye all right?"

"Of course." She forced a smile and squeezed Effie's fingers before pulling back, then dabbed away the gruesome memory and the dampness on her face with the back of her hand. "I am fine. Just a bit melancholy, though I've no right to be. This hair will make a beautiful fob for Father's watch, and I am grateful you took the time today to help me snip it. I can't wait to see the smile on his face when we exchange gifts on Christmas Eve."

Effie cocked her head, studying her. Apparently satisfied, she bent and collected the locks from the floor. "So, when are ye goin' to tell me?"

Frowning, Mina angled her head one way then another, studying Effie's trimming. "Tell you what?"

"About your plans for Christmas in the country."

Her hands dropped. So did her jaw. "You know? How?"

Setting the hair on the vanity, Effie lifted a brow at her in the mirror. "I ran into Miss Whymsy late yesterday at the milliner's. She were buying a bit o' lace to dress up her hat. Ain't no call for such fanciness just to be volunteering at the institute, so I got it out of her that she's attending you on a little jaunt to the country for Christmas."

She shook her head. The woman was a wonder. "Effie, you could get a marble statue to spill its secrets."

"Ha! I ain't that good. That's all what she told me. I don't know where yer goin' or why, or how you even managed to talk Miss Whymsy into taking a leave from her volunteering. She just said, and I quote, 'Miss Scott and I are venturing out on a small excursion to the countryside. Do be a dear and check on Miss Minton for me in the meantime.'" Effie picked up a brush and tapped it against one palm.

Mina smirked. "I suppose you won't leave here today without me filling you in?"

A brilliant grin brightened Effie's plain face. "Well, it'll take me a good few minutes to style yer hair, and ye've nothing better to do while ye sit there."

"Very well." She sighed as Effie began brushing. "Remember that dinner I told you about, the one at Will's Uncle Barlow's?"

"Aye."

"I thought that would be the end of it, but it wasn't. Now Uncle Barlow has invited us to share Christmas with him in the country."

The brush stopped midstroke next to her ear, and Effie's wide-eyed gaze met hers in the mirror. "But what of the Christmas Eve celebration here at the Golden Egg? It's tradition! Ye can't miss that."

"You sound just like Father. But not to worry, for I shall return by then. Father insisted, and Will said he'd figure out a way to explain it to his uncle."

"Hmm." Effie ran the brush through the rest of her hair, then set it down and picked up a few pins. "Well, at least you're done with the pretend bride business, eh?"

She bit her lip.

"Mina?"

"Sort of," she mumbled.

"How can ye be a 'sort of' bride?" Effie tugged a hank of hair into place and shoved in a pin. "What has your father to say about that?"

Guilt scraped her soul every bit as much as the jab of Effie's next hairpin. Neither she nor Will had mentioned anything about the charade to Father. She couldn't imagine what he'd say. It had been hard enough trying to convince Miss Whymsy to go along with the sham-marriage story until Will had a chance to speak with his uncle. Once the gravity of Uncle Barlow's situation had been explained—plus the fact that Will had asked her father for permission to court her, moving them in the general direction of matrimony—Miss Whymsy had grudgingly agreed. The old lady had vowed, however, that she'd not lie outright. And neither would Mina.

She sat taller and tilted her head, giving Effie a better reach to finish pinning up her hair. "William promised he'd tell his uncle the truth of things soon after we arrive. . .and he asked my father last Saturday if he might court me. So maybe, perhaps, I might be a real bride in the near future."

"Oh, love! How wonderful."

It was. She kept telling herself that. But she couldn't stop the frown weighting her brow.

Effie stooped, staring face-to-face in the mirror with her. "Why do ye look as if it's not so wonderful?"

A sigh to rip a hole in the universe gushed out of her. Would voicing her doubts make them real? *Oh, God, please no.* But the determined gleam in Effie's brown eyes would not be denied.

"I don't know if it's real, Effie. Does William truly care for me, or is this just an act to save his uncle? Not that I mind saving his uncle, but. . .oh, I don't know. I suppose I feel like a character in a book, not knowing how the plot will twist—and am unable to flip to the last page to find out."

Effie shook her head. "But your story is already written, and it does have a happy ending. Are we not promised heaven when we die?"

"It's not the dying part that concerns me. It's the in-between now and then."

"Ahh, love...if we knew how things would turn out, then there'd be no need for faith, aye? My mother—God rest her—always told me to think of eternity, then live backward from that. Such a view has a way o' whittlin' down our current troubles to a size we can crumple up into a ball and toss aside."

The words sank in deep, convicting and healing. Her friend was right. What had become of her faith? *Oh, Lord, forgive me.*

Reaching up, she patted Effie's arm. "Thank you for the reminder. What would I do without you?"

"Well, for one, you might have more hair on yer head." With a purse of her lips, Effie straightened and finished with the last of her pins. "There. What do ye think?"

Tipping her head, she narrowed her eyes and studied every angle. Not one bit of shorter hair remained uncovered. "You are a miracle worker."

"Not really, but I happen to know the Giver of all miracles, and ye can bet I'll be on my knees every mornin' praying for ye while ye're gone."

"Thank you. I have a feeling I'll be needing a miracle or two, especially if I'm going to get this watch fob finished before I leave. That's only a little over a week and a half, and it's not like I can devote all my time to such a project."

"Knowing yer nimble fingers, ye'll have it done in a trice." Effie swiped up the old coin she'd given her weeks ago from where it sat on the vanity. She held the bit of gold out on an open palm. "And for heaven's sake, tuck this coin into yer pocket and carry it with ye at all times. Ye just might need to give someone a second chance at that estate, especially if Mr. Barlow's cousins are to be there as well."

Indeed. She wrapped her fingers around the coin. Taking courage from her friend's words of faith and the piece of gold in her hand, she did feel ready for her upcoming adventure. Mostly.

CHAPTER NINETEEN

The light snowfall, which had feathered his
schoolroom windows on the Thursday,
still lingered in the air, and was falling white.
Our Mutual Friend

Outside the carriage window, snowflakes floated. Some seemed
to hang suspended. Others languished to the ground. Mina
huffed on the glass, then rubbed away the condensation for a
clearer view. She'd never been to Essex, nor witnessed such a magical sight. The road to Uncle Barlow's estate wound through a
wooded countryside, slowly being tucked in beneath a light counterpane of white.

Would this be the best Christmas ever?

Will rode on horseback, trotting ahead of the carriage, his words
of a fortnight ago yet echoed in her mind as she settled back against
the seat. Judging by the fairyland outside, his "best Christmas" was
off to a good start.

She slipped a sideways glance at Miss Whymsy, who peered out
the window on her side of the carriage. The older lady seemed as
mesmerized by the wonderland outside as she.

"God's artistry never ceases to amaze me." Her friend turned
from the window. "Though my bones don't appreciate the chill, I
can't help but revel in the beauty. Oh, how I've missed this."

"You've been to Essex?"

A curious smile lifted Miss Whymsy's lips, as if she savored the
aftertaste of a treasured secret. "I served in a country home not far

from here. A bit more north though, I should think. Ahh, but those were happy memories."

Yet as the carriage rolled along, the woman's smile faded to a shadow.

Mina patted her friend's leg, hoping to impart some kind of comfort. "Pardon my noticing, but you don't seem happy, thinking of those times."

"I suppose I should have said bittersweet." The blue-green in Miss Whymsy's eyes deepened to a shade of hopeful despair, a contradiction that raised hundreds of questions.

And Mina couldn't keep from letting one slip out. "In what respect? That is, if you don't mind talking about it."

"Not at all, for therein does Mr. Hargrave yet live."

The carriage wheels dipped into a rut, giving her a good excuse for the sudden gasp and grasp of the seat. Had Miss Whymsy a past lover?

"Mr. Hargrave?" Mina rolled the name out like an invitation, hoping the woman would share more. "I've never heard you make mention of him."

"There's never been an occasion, I suppose, until now. Believe it or not, I was young once, like you, and thoroughly taken with a Mr. Roger Hargrave—not unlike your affection for the dashing Mr. Barlow."

Mina shifted on the seat, stifling the urge to fan her face though the air was chill. By faith! Why could she never master the flush that always accompanied the mention of Will?

"But as I was saying," Miss Whymsy continued, "Roger Hargrave was the most dashing gentleman I'd ever met. So handsome. So upstanding. He was the younger brother of the earl in whose home I served."

The older lady leaned closer, eyes twinkling, her trademark lavender scent wafting like summer on this wintry day. "We were engaged to be married."

This time her jaw did drop. "You were married?"

"No. You see. . ." For a moment, Miss Whymsy's gaze drifted back to the window, but Mina got the distinct impression the older lady didn't see the snow-laced trees or wintry landscape. She likely wandered in a far-off land of memory—until the woman drew in a deep breath and once again faced her. "My Roger was a military man, called off for one last stint in the Indies where he succumbed to a fever. . .a week before he was to return."

"Oh!" Mina recoiled, her hat bumping against the back of the carriage. "How dreadful."

"It was, but don't fret on my account." Miss Whymsy lifted her chin, her breath coming out in little white puffs. "Though Roger's been gone these thirty years, I have learned to cherish the pain of his absence."

"Cherish pain?" She shook her head, but even that didn't put any order to the curious thought. "I don't understand."

"You see, my dear, real joy is not found in the best moments of life, but in trusting that God is making the best of *every* moment. . . even those as dreadful as death."

What an odd sentiment. Mina sank deeper into the seat cushion, her thoughts taking a dive into Miss Whymsy's logic. How could it possibly have been the best for her to lose her mother at only seven years of age? Was it best that she'd wept for years on end and her father grieved alone every night? Or maybe—*perhaps*—had she been so caught up in the losing that she'd given no thought to the trusting part of the equation?

"I can see you're puzzled. Let me try to explain it a bit better." The governess inside Miss Whymsy emerged in the straightening of her shoulders. "I believe that when God permits pain, it is for the purpose of allowing something new to be born inside of us. I am not the same person I would be had Roger lived—and I trust my clever Creator that I am the better for it."

"So you're saying," Mina thought aloud, "that if my mother had lived, I wouldn't be the person I am today."

"Exactly. Oh, don't get me wrong, my dear." Miss Whymsy reached over and squeezed her hand. "I am in no way trying to negate how awful it was for you to experience the loss of your mother. I am simply saying that one must cherish all moments in life, happy or sad, for when you are older, memories are ofttimes all you have left."

Mina's heart broke, especially thinking of Miss Whymsy sitting by herself in front of the tiny hearth in her chamber, a tea tray set for one on the small table beside her, alone with naught but her memories. "Is it so very awful, living alone?"

"La!" the old lady chuckled, the ruffled edge of her bonnet bobbing with the movement. "God's children are never truly alone— especially in a world filled with books. I daresay you know that, hmm?"

They fell silent then and remained so until the carriage slowed. The horses stopped in front of a three-story, white-stone building, looking as merry as the snowflakes that danced about it. Vines wrapped brown arms around the structure in a loving embrace, and were it spring, no doubt green leaves would offer a stunning show against the backdrop. As her gaze landed on two bay windows curving out on either side of the front door, her smile returned in full force. What a perfect place to curl up with a book.

She turned to Miss Whymsy and rested her hand on the lady's arm. "Thank you for coming along with me. I hope you shall enjoy your stay here."

"I am sure—"

Just then the carriage door flung wide, and instead of the expected footman offering a hand, Uncle Barlow's grey-tufted head poked into the carriage. "I've been waiting for you—oh? What's this?" His eyes widened as his gaze landed on Miss Whymsy. "*Two* lovely ladies? How grand! M'ladies, my castle awaits." He backed out and held the door wide.

"Actually, my dear," Miss Whymsy quirked a brow toward her. "I have a feeling I shall enjoy my visit here *very* much."

Chapter Twenty

There is no playing fast and loose with the truth,
in any game, without growing the worse for it.
Little Dorrit

Will handed over his horse's lead to a stableboy, then patted the mount on the neck. The ride from Bishop's Stortford to Uncle's estate had been refreshing, reminding him how much he missed the sweetness of air unsullied by coal smoke and humanity.

"Mind you rub this fellow down good and have his left foreleg checked. He seemed to be favoring it."

"Aye, sir." The boy dipped his head.

Wheeling about, Will strode to the front door of Uncle Barlow's country home, his footsteps muffled by the thin layer of snow. Ahead, Uncle held out both arms, Mina's gloved hand perched on one, and Miss Whymsy's curled around the other. Uncle threw back his head, his laughter jolly in the greyness of the late afternoon.

Following their heels, Will entered the large foyer, already decorated for Christmas, and breathed in the scent of fresh greenery, beeswax candles, and hundreds of memories. Ahead rose the staircase where he and Percy used to race down the banisters on Christmas morn—until the year Percy had fallen and his nursemaid had put a stop to that. To his left, the door to the sitting room. How many summer holidays had he hidden behind the settee to avoid having to ride with his cousin? For Percy had ever been the worst horseman on the face of the planet. All walk and no gallop.

Shoving aside the memories, he caught up to Mina and helped

her out of her wraps. Uncle Barlow assisted Miss Whymsy, and they loaded down a servant with cloaks, hats, and mufflers.

"Oh, my!" Mina breathed out as her wide-eyed gaze drifted from the holly-and-ivy garland along the stairway to a bowl of clove-studded oranges on a nearby table. "You've decorated early for Christmas."

Uncle Barlow gathered one of her hands in both of his, patting the top of it. "I thought that since we'd not be here for the actual holiday, why not decorate now? It was so thoughtful of you, my dear, to have invited us all to your father's Christmas Eve gala at the Golden Egg. I own I've never been there, yet William tells me the oyster stew is not to be missed. And I cannot think of a more perfect venue or time in which to announce who my heir will be."

"Th–thank you," Mina stammered. As soon as Uncle released her hand and Miss Whymsy claimed his attention, she shot Will a narrow-eyed glance and a whisper. "What did you—?"

"Sorry," he whispered back, adding a sheepish smile that he hoped was convincing. "It was the only way I could think of for us to leave here by Christmas."

Her brows pulled together. "But—"

Whatever rejoinder she intended died on her lips as Alice and Percy descended the stairway. Will stifled a smirk. Saved by his cousins. That was a first.

"Well." Percy sniffed as he joined Will's side. "I see you've arrived."

In spite of his cousin's rancor, he couldn't help but smile. Some things never changed. In an odd sort of way, Percy's predictability was at least familiar, like donning a ratty woolen jumper, all scratchy and smelling of mothballs, yet altogether a necessity to the feeling of having arrived home.

"Good afternoon to you too, Percy. Alice." He nodded in greeting.

Alice bypassed him and closed in on Mina. "Good afternoon,

Mina. I hope your journey wasn't too taxing, though by the looks of you, it likely was. I see you've brought along your mother."

Pink flushed Mina's cheeks. "Oh, but this is not my mother. This is one of my dearest friends, Miss Whymsy. Miss Whymsy, please meet Alice Barlow, wife of Percival Barlow, Will's cousins."

The older lady bowed her head. "Pleased to meet you, Mrs. Barlow, Mr. Barlow."

"A friend, you say?" Alice's green eyes narrowed as she swept her gaze over Miss Whymsy—and apparently found her lacking, judging by the perfect pout on her lips. She whirled back to Mina. "You brought along an uninvited guest? How bold. One might almost get the impression you felt the need for a chaperone."

An alarm gonged inside Will's head. If Alice continued that line of reasoning, she might draw a very revealing picture. He opened his mouth—

But Uncle Barlow charged ahead, collecting Miss Whymsy's hand and placing it on his arm. "I assure you, Alice, had I known Mina was acquainted with such a delightful lady, I would have invited her straightaway myself. Miss Whymsy, allow me to escort you to the sitting room, where you can wait for a chamber to be readied."

At her consent, they both disappeared out of the foyer.

Percy sidled closer to Will. "A very clever scheme, Cousin."

Ignoring the man, Will swept out his hand toward Mina. Sometimes the best defense was to change the subject. "Mina? How about I show you the house?"

She stepped to his side.

But Percy blocked their passage. "It won't work, you know."

Afternoon light glinted off Percy's spectacles, drilling a beam into his eyes, and he blinked. Clearly there'd be no putting off the man. "I have no idea what you're talking about."

"Bringing the old lady to distract Uncle. You think she can make up for your dodgy past?"

Beside him, Mina tensed. Blast his cousin for always planting doubt in her mind. "No, I do not," he said through clenched teeth. "But if Uncle enjoys Miss Whymsy's company, why begrudge him a little happiness at Christmas?"

"There is something not right about this." Alice tapped a finger against her lips. "Something I intend to find out."

Mina huddled closer to his side, and he stretched out his arm, drawing her near.

And at that moment, Uncle Barlow strolled out of the sitting room, chuckling. He clapped his hands and rubbed them together. "This shall be the merriest of Christmases. I feel it in my bones." He stopped in front of the group and nodded to Will. "Why don't you see Mina up to the blue room and you can both refresh from your travels. We'll meet for dinner at seven o'clock."

Will waited for further instruction, but Uncle Barlow turned, apparently dismissing them.

"And to what room shall my things be delivered?" he asked.

Without turning back, Uncle waggled his fingers in the air. "Why, the blue room of course."

Percy and Alice give him a queer look—but their confusion was nothing compared to the apprehension in Mina's large eyes as she blinked up at him.

He tugged his collar, fighting for air. Of course he'd be expected to share a bedchamber with his wife.

CHAPTER TWENTY-ONE

Death doesn't change us more than life.
The Old Curiosity Shop

Mina stepped into paradise.

She'd read of bedchambers like this. Walls papered with blue velveteen. Windows overlooking a wonderland of snow-encrusted tree branches. A merry fire glowed in the hearth, and thick rugs added warmth to the room. On one wall was a mahogany desk with a matching chair. Near the fireplace sat two wingbacks stuffed full enough that one might sleep the night through in them without a crick in the neck. A small table rested against another wall with a full tea set. Against the third wall stood a vanity filled with bottles and brushes and a mirror that bounced back light from the windows. But as her gaze landed on the bed—canopied and ruffled and with mattresses so high, a stepstool stood nearby—her stomach twisted.

That bed was clearly meant for two.

Flames shot from her stomach to her cheeks. She whirled to face Will. "You cannot possibly stay in here with me. You must speak with your uncle today. Now!"

"Shh." He lifted a finger to his lips and closed the door behind him. "Percy and Alice weren't far behind us."

She retreated a step. He followed. He wasn't seriously thinking of spending the afternoon with her here? Alone? This was taking things too far. Far too far. A hero would not even think such a thing. "This is indecent."

She sidestepped him, but he blocked her.

"Mina, you have my word. I will tell my uncle as soon as the opportunity presents itself, but he's clearly preoccupied with your Miss Whymsy for the moment. Let's give him time to get her settled. We've only just arrived."

"Well you cannot remain with me behind a closed door for the afternoon."

"I know." He rubbed the back of his neck. Was he as knotted up about the situation then? "I shall think of something."

"What?"

"I don't know." His hand dropped. "But if nothing else, there's a spare room at the end of this corridor. I'll wait until no one's about, then slip off down there."

"If my father hears of this—"

"He won't. Mina, please." He closed the distance between them and rested his hands on her shoulders, giving them a little squeeze. "We ought not give Percy and Alice anything more to wonder about, hmm? All will be well. I promise. Try to relax."

Relax? When she stood in a bedchamber alone with Will Barlow? Riding in a carriage with the man had been scandalous enough, but this was immoral. She pulled away.

"Mina, I am sorry, truly. I should have seen this coming, and I didn't. Forgive me?" He dipped his head, looking at her through his lashes. A lad with his hand caught in the sweets jar couldn't have looked more contrite.

She sighed. How was she to stay cross with such a look? "Very well."

"That's my girl." His head perked up, and he strode to the door. After a glance into the corridor, he looked over his shoulder at her. "All's clear. Rest up. Your trunk will soon be brought 'round, and I shall meet you downstairs later for dinner. Agreed?"

She nodded, for there was nothing more she could do save storm out of there and tell Will's uncle herself.

As soon as Will shut the door behind him, she wandered the room a bit, trailing a finger over much of the finery. Memorizing it all. Was this how Esther Summerson had felt when she'd first arrived at Bleak House?

A yawn stretched her jaw, and the quilted counterpane on the big bed called to her. After travelling all day, it would be lovely to close her eyes, just for a few minutes.

But by the time a rap on the door jolted her awake and a white-aproned maid peeked her head in, more than minutes had passed. Darkness filled the room.

"Might I help you dress for dinner, ma'am?"

She blinked, fighting the urge to look over her shoulder to see to whom the maid offered her services, though it could be none other than her—and that sent a thrill through her. She smiled at the woman as the servant scurried about the room, lighting lamps. "Thank you, but no need. I shall manage quite well on my own."

"As you wish, ma'am."

The maid was followed by a footman with her small trunk hefted up on one shoulder. He set it down next to a large wardrobe, then with a bob of his head, exited as well.

Mina crossed to her trunk and lifted out her dresses. There were only two—her very best—and she frowned at them both. By the third night, when she'd have to repeat one, surely Alice would have something to say about it. But perhaps by then, the truth would be out, and there'd be no reason to stay any longer.

She hung up one dress, then worked her way into the other. By the time she pinned up her hair, she smiled at her reflection in the mirror, satisfied that she looked her best, leastwise for tonight. After one more visit to her trunk, where she pulled out a small pouch containing the second-chance coin, she tucked the bit of gold into her pocket. She might not need it tonight, but when dining with Will's cousins, one never knew.

Stepping out into the corridor, she shivered. The air was far more chill than her chamber, so she upped her pace and descended the stairs to ground level. Surely the dining room was here somewhere, though she should have asked Will the location.

She passed the sitting room, and near the end of another passageway, two doors stood open. Golden light poured out of each. Could be either, so for no other reason than a whim, she ducked into the door on the right.

Then gasped. Books lined three walls, and on the fourth, at least twenty-five pairs of eyes stared back at her. Drawn toward the gilt-framed portraits, she padded inside and wandered from picture to picture.

One was surely a dark-haired Uncle Barlow with his apple-cheeks shaven clean and face smoothed of wrinkles. She cocked her head. He might almost be. . .yes, with that straight nose and strong jawline, the resemblance to Will was stunning.

To the left of Uncle Barlow's portrait was a shadow-faced fellow with a severe brow and overly large eyes. The man was seated, and beside him posed a bony woman in a brown, empire-waisted gown. Both frowned. Each looked as if they'd prefer to run off to another canvas rather than live immortally together in this painting. Were these Percy's parents?

She sidestepped over to the other side of Uncle Barlow's picture, and her breath hitched as she looked into Will's eyes. The hair on this man was a shade darker, but all the same, the features matched Will's exactly. . .save for one thing. There was a certain sadness to this portrait. The kind that called out from the years like a whisper from a grave. She stepped closer, gooseflesh rising on her arms. Was this Will's father? And if so, why was his mother not featured here as well?

"I thought I might find you here."

A deep voice turned her around, and she slapped a hand to her chest. "Uncle Barlow, you startled me."

"Sorry, my dear, but no need to fear in this house. To my

knowledge, there are no ghosts—Christmas or otherwise— roaming about. Once a Barlow is dead, he is well and truly dead." He chuckled as he crossed the rug to stand next to her. "I see you've found William's father, and no wonder, for my nephew is the very image of my brother Edward. Both of them too handsome for their own good."

"He is so young here. He can't be much older than Will is now."

"True, and this is how I shall always remember him. Carefree. Laughter at the ready. Holding the world in two hands and tossing it about like a ball. I admired that about him, though I never spoke it aloud, for elder brothers rarely do." Uncle Barlow cleared his throat, then murmured, "In my quieter moments, I yet miss him keenly."

Sorrow thickened his words. He must've loved his brother very much to still feel such strong emotion. Was that why he'd given Will a second chance, perhaps? Had it been some kind of offering of honor to a lost brother?

Pulling her gaze from the portrait, she turned to Uncle Barlow. "What happened to Will's father?"

"It is a sad story, one best told while seated." He turned and sank into one of the chairs near the hearth, then waited for her to take the other. "Edward was the youngest of us three Barlow boys. And as you know, the youngest often are the wiliest. I suppose they have to be, to keep up with their elders. But Edward was more than that. He was a sunburst on a clouded day, always ready with a laugh, and oh, what a charmer. He could lure a penny from a miser's purse with nothing more than one of his grins."

She smiled. "He sounds like William."

"Indeed." Uncle Barlow grinned as well, but then as memories played over his face, his mirth faded. "He was."

"What happened to him?" she whispered.

For a long while, Uncle Barlow stared into the fire, saying nothing. Did he even know she was still in the room? Just at the point when she was sure he wouldn't answer, he pushed up from his chair and stood with his back to the hearth, flipping up his suit tails to warm his backside. "My brother Edward died not long after your William was born. Both he and William's mother were taken by a fever. It is God's grace alone that little William survived."

"How awful." She pulled the words out of a great storehouse of sorrow. The pain of growing up without a mother was bad enough, but to not have a father either?

"You sound as if you've held hands with loss yourself, my dear."

Shoving down a rising melancholy, she nodded, eager to change the subject. "Uncle Barlow, I wonder if William spoke with you this afternoon?"

"I'm afraid I was a bit indisposed." A chuckle rumbled in his chest. "Your Miss Whymsy is delightful, and I confess to overindulging in her company. I took her on a tour of the entire grounds."

"I see." So, the old fellow *still* didn't know the truth. She pressed her lips flat.

Uncle Barlow returned to his chair. "What was it William wanted to speak to me about?"

Absently, she ran her hands along her legs, smoothing wrinkles from her gown. Would Will be very cross if she told his uncle herself? But was this not the perfect opportunity? And they had agreed he should know.

"Uncle Barlow," she began before she could change her mind. "There is something you need to know about Will and me."

"Oh? And what is that?"

Trying not to think of the disappointment in his eyes when he found out about the deception, she pressed on. "We are not actually—"

"There you are. I thought as much." Percy's voice boomed through the open door, and they turned. Will's cousin frowned at her, then shifted his gaze to Uncle Barlow. "We are all waiting on you, Uncle, and have been for some time."

The old fellow patted her knee. "We shall have to continue this later, my dear." Rising, he held out his arm and winked, speaking for her alone. "It promises to be a lively evening, for I've taken the liberty of seating Miss Whymsy next to me. I don't suppose Alice shall like it, but then neither Alice nor Percy seem to like much of anything, eh?"

She rose and took his arm, fingering her pocket with her free hand. Maybe she would need that second-chance coin tonight after all.

For hopefully she'd get a second chance to tell Uncle Barlow the truth.

CHAPTER TWENTY-TWO

Never close your lips to those whom you
have already opened your heart.
Charles Dickens

The evening stretched into a long, sharp dagger and took a deadlier turn when Uncle Barlow and Miss Whymsy decided to retire early. Something about overdoing the day. Will grimaced as he set down his untouched glass of sherry. After parrying Alice's cutting remarks and deflecting Percy's verbal swipes, he'd had enough. "Come along, Mina. It's been a long day for us as well." He offered her his hand, then glanced at his cousins. "Good night."

"Hmm. Perhaps," Percy drawled.

Ignoring whatever the scoundrel had in mind, Will led Mina from the room more exhausted than he'd ever been. Normally he would have laughed off such vitriol. Dodged his cousins' jabs as cleverly as he might a bucket of slop being dumped out a Cheapside window. But when Mina became the sole target of such venom, he'd had no choice but to usher her out before he popped Percy in the nose.

As they strolled toward the staircase, Mina's gaze sought his. "You know you cannot stay in my chamber."

"Of course not." He winked down at her, hoping the lighthearted action would calm her fears.

"But where will you sleep?"

"Don't fret. I've got things under control." For a moment, he wished he had drunk that sherry, if for nothing more than to wash away the bitter taste his words left in his mouth. Under control? Ha! A spinning kaleidoscope couldn't have been more crazed than this topsy-turvy day.

Mina paused and turned to him at the foot of the stairs. "Do you suppose your uncle would mind if I brought a book with me to bed?"

"I should think he'd be delighted and"—he leaned toward her and tapped her on the nose—"would want to hear your thoughts on it when you're finished."

He wheeled about and led her to the library, where she seemed more than at home. He watched her as she roamed from shelf to shelf, her delight doing strange things to his heart. She belonged here, surrounded by books as if they were old friends. Running her fingers along each shelf, she'd pause with a mysterious twitch to her lips, and for some odd reason, he wished this moment to never end. Was this how it was for God to gaze upon His creation as they enjoyed His gifts?

As she passed near a wall sconce, soft light teased out the coppery glimmers in her hair, all done up and begging for release. How long would those locks fall? How silky the feel? His fingers curled in reflex and—sweet blessed heavens. . .what *was* he thinking?

Finally, she pulled a book off of a shelf, and a little coo caught in her throat. Judging by the way she cradled the thing to her breast, she'd found a favorite. As she rambled back to where he waited for her at the door, her smile faltered for a moment—when her gaze slid to the portrait of his father.

"Will. . ." she bit her lip as she drew close to him, bringing the sweet scent of the rosemary water she'd freshened up with. "I hope you don't mind, but your uncle told me the sad tale of your father and mother earlier today."

He stiffened. Father. . .*and mother?* What could the old fellow possibly say about her? "What do you mean?"

"How they died of a fever. I had no idea you grew up without knowing either of them. It was hard enough losing my mother as a child. I can't imagine not having my father around. I am sorry for your loss."

Compassion shimmered in Mina's eyes, and the fish he'd eaten at dinner flipped in his gut. All the deceptions, the secrets, knotted into a great net, trapping him and squeezing the breath from his lungs. This had to stop. Surely he owed Mina some morsels of truth—despite his mother's wishes. Besides, it wasn't as if he were telling Uncle Barlow.

"Mina, there's something my uncle didn't tell you, because he doesn't know it himself. But I feel I must be honest with you, for you've suffered enough untruths at my request. My mother is, well... she's still alive, though for how much longer, I am not certain. She is very ill."

"She's not dead?" The words rolled from her lips as if she tasted each one and couldn't decide whether she liked the flavor. "While I am happy for you that your mother is yet among the living, why does your uncle think—why do you *allow* him to think—she is dead? I don't understand."

Of course she didn't. He'd barely understood it himself that day six months ago when a solicitor had tracked him down and told him the unbelievable details. Reaching, he kneaded a rock-hard muscle on his shoulder. "It is a complicated story," he said at length.

She merely shrugged. "I am well familiar with such tales, for are not all our lives a tangled heap of joy and sorrow? Still, if you'd rather not tell it, I understand."

The pity in her eyes made his heart skip a beat. Had ever a more compassionate woman graced this earth?

Leaning back against the doorjamb, he folded his arms. He'd already relayed the story to Fitz. There could be no harm in sharing it with Mina as well, for his mother had only bade him not to reveal the details to his family.

"My father," he began, "was the youngest brother, and as such, was indulged. Overmuch. And to his detriment, I might add. Though my grandfather urged him to go into the church, he could not give up his artistic bent or his dream to become a renowned painter. He talked Grandfather—or rather Grandmother—into allowing him to study for a year in France amongst the masters. It was there he met my mother."

Mina's nose bunched. "This doesn't sound so complicated."

"This is where it takes a turn." He sighed. How to put this delicately? "While staying as a guest in the house of one of his former schoolmate's relatives, he became enamored with the gentleman's daughter. He asked to paint her, and she accepted. During those long sessions, alone, his admiration of her turned into an indiscretion."

"Oh." Pink blossomed on Mina's cheeks, and for a moment, he considered if he should continue.

Unfolding his arms, he paced the rug in front of the door. Better to tell the rest without making eye contact. "When my mother told my father she was with child, he knew he had to do the right thing and marry her. But she was French. And in his English family's eyes, that would be a mark against her. Were they to find out she was also bearing his child, they'd both be outcasts."

Mina's breath caught. "So what happened?"

"He brought her home immediately, intending to marry in the Anglican church before anyone knew. But while doing a fitting for my mother's dress, a servant noticed her thickening middle and went straight to Grandfather. Needless to say, it did not go over well. Grandfather allowed the marriage to continue to give the child—me—a name, but he swore my parents to secrecy and banned them from his household immediately following the ceremony."

"How awful."

"It was." He stopped his mad pacing and faced her. "They moved to London, where they took up a shabby existence. My father scrabbled to sell miniature portraits while my mother tried desperately to get jobs tutoring French. Shortly after my birth, my father took ill and died. My mother, alone in a foreign country, with a babe and no means to support herself, decided to bring me back to my father's family and plead for Grandfather to take me in, for she couldn't return to her home with a child born far too soon after their marriage. Grandfather agreed. I was whisked off to be cared for by a hired nurse until I could be weaned and questions wouldn't be asked. He let everyone believe—even me—that my mother had died of a fever alongside my father."

"Oh, Will. . ." Mina's words shivered on the air. "I am so sorry. I shouldn't have asked."

He shrugged. "Well, there is somewhat of a happy ending. I hope, at any rate. When my mother recently fell ill, hanging by a thread onto life, she sent a solicitor to find me, which he did, thank God. I have been to see her, and I hope—and pray—that by moving her here, I can care for her, and she'll soon recover."

"I pray so too." Her blue gaze met his. "Thank you for telling me."

Nodding, he swept his hand toward the door. "It is getting late. I should see you up to your room."

He pivoted and strode past the threshold—and came face-to-face with Percy.

Blast! If his cousin had heard any of his tale. . .his hands curled into fists. "How long have you been standing there?" he ground out.

A slow smile spread across Percy's face. "Long enough. Good night, Cousin."

Percy wheeled about and stalked down the corridor.

"Oh, dear." Coming up from behind, Mina rested her hand on his sleeve. "He'll tell your uncle, won't he?"

His shoulders sagged, but a steely determination shored up his soul. Though his mother had asked him otherwise, there was nothing to be done for it now. "Not if I tell him first."

And he would. He'd seek out Uncle Barlow first thing on the morrow and tell him everything or die in the trying.

Chapter Twenty-Three

There is nothing so strong or safe in an emergency
of life as the simple truth.
Charles Dickens

He'd meant to talk to his uncle, truly he had, but the next day passed in a blur of festive activities—and never once had Uncle been without Miss Whymsy at his side. Morning. Afternoon. Evening. All the events had chafed like a damp woolen muffler, rubbing Will's conscience so raw that by the time he escorted Mina up the stairway to her chamber well after nightfall, he could hardly stand himself. Now that he was finally ready to divulge everything to his uncle, it seemed as if the powers of hell conspired against his bringing the truth to light.

At the top of the stairs, Mina leaned close to him and lowered her voice. "Have you spoken to your uncle?"

"Trust me, I tried, but not yet. It seems your Miss Whymsy is a particular favorite of his. The two were inseparable all day."

"I noticed. I've never seen her so happy, so. . .animated, I suppose." A brief smile flickered on her lips, then just as soon faded. "Though I am sorry you weren't able to corner Uncle Barlow because of her."

"Well, the good news is that Percy wasn't able to either." He offered his arm, and they continued down the corridor toward the blue room. "As near as I can tell, that is."

"Which is a bit strange, I think. Your cousin seems the type to relish a good tattling, no matter if your uncle were occupied or not."

"I know. That does have me concerned." He scrubbed his face with his free hand. Percy had never been able to keep a secret—especially one as tantalizing as this. So why now?

"I pray you'll have better luck tomorrow." Mina smiled up at him. "And I'll try to detain Miss Whymsy for you."

"Actually, I still have a chance to speak with my uncle tonight. It's his habit to record the day's activities in a journal he keeps in his study. I'm not sure if it's the writing he enjoys more or the cherry tobacco he uses in his pipe while composing." He winked down at her—and was rewarded with a blush that pinked Mina's cheeks to a most becoming shade.

"Well, despite everything, it was a lovely day. The sleigh ride. Meeting some of the tenants. Oh, and the drinking chocolate afterwards. Sublime!" Her eyes closed and her mouth moved as if she were savoring it all over again.

He couldn't help but chuckle. Such innocence. Such beauty. A sweet combination of all that was lovely and right. His mirth fled, replaced with a sobering revelation. Not only would he never tire of spending time with Mina—he didn't want his time with her to end.

Her eyes popped open, and she arched a brow. "If you don't mind, I shall have to steal that recipe and bring it home to Martha. What an addition it would be to Father's Christmas celebration. It might even outshine his oyster stew."

He stopped at her chamber door and tapped her on the nose. "No thievery involved. You have my blessing to ask Cook for it."

He opened her door and stood aside, but she hesitated on the threshold, apparently lost in thought. Fine little creases marred her brow.

"A farthing for your thoughts?" he asked.

"I. . .well. . ." She sighed as if the weight of the world were hers to carry.

He stepped closer, alarmed yet instantly ready to fight whatever dragon tormented her so. "Tell me."

She peered up at him, her blue eyes almost greenish, so pure was her anguish. "I am concerned about the Christmas party, what with your uncle and cousins planning on attending. Father doesn't know we've been playing the part of being married, and were they to hint at anything, well. . .if my father finds out, I—"

He laid a finger against her lips, and his knees nearly buckled from the softness that met his touch. "Stop right there. If the rest of the evening goes as promised, I shall have the matter taken care of by morning. You are not to lose one bit of sleep over this. Promise?"

For a moment she wavered, then her gaze brightened back to normal and the trust shining in those blue ponds did strange things to his gut. He lowered his hand to keep from pulling her into his arms.

"I promise." A small smile curved her mouth.

"Right then, off with you. See you at breakfast."

She nodded and crossed into her chamber, then turned with her hand on the door. "Good night, Will."

Ahh, but she was a picture, standing there with lamplight bathing her in an angelic glow. It took him several tries just to get out a simple goodbye. "Good night."

Turning on his heel, he fled down the corridor. It was either that or give in to the urge to kiss her senseless. He upped his pace as he descended the stairs, then swung around the staircase and strode toward Uncle's study. The sooner he got this over with, the better. Bracing himself for a long night of explaining, he stepped through the open door. "Uncle Barlow, sorry to disturb you, but there's something important I need to. . ."

His words stumbled to a halt as two grey heads turned to look at him from across the room. A lively blaze in the hearth cast light on the figures seated on the sofa—his uncle *and* Miss Whymsy. He shoved down a groan. Ought not a woman of Miss Whymsy's age be abed? What on earth could they possibly be talking about now when they'd been locked in conversation all the blessed day?

Uncle Barlow beckoned with one hand. "Come and join us William. Miss Whymsy here is just telling me about her volunteer work at an institute I'd never heard of. Quite interesting. You may learn a thing or two."

"I. . .uh. . ." Clamping his mouth shut, he gritted his teeth. What to do? Stay and listen, wait out whatever the older lady had to say—which could take hours, as elders generally got sidetracked frequently and for long periods. Or leave now and have a go at Uncle first thing in the morning?

"Yes, do come join us, Mr. Barlow. If you're half as enthralled as your uncle at my stories, I daresay I could regale you until day-break." Laughter warbled past the lady's lips.

Just as he'd thought. The two of them had settled in and would make a very long night of it, and by the time it wrapped up, no doubt Uncle would be too weary for the weight of the sordid truth Will must tell him.

"I thank you, but—" He forced a small yawn. "I didn't realize the hour. Perhaps, Uncle, I might speak with you straight off in the morning?"

"Of course. Any time, my boy. And a hearty good night to you."

The two grey heads turned to once again face each other. Defeated, Will shuffled out of the room. Apparently the truth battle was one he'd have to wage the following day.

He retraced his steps up to the first floor, then stalked down the dimly lit corridor. A light still glowed beneath Mina's door, and he couldn't help but grin as he imagined her taking down her hair and brushing it until the reddish glints shone like fire.

Passing on, he took care to edge toward the far side of the wall as he drew close to his cousins' door. No light glowed in the crack near their threshold. Good. Then neither Percy nor Alice would hear his footsteps as he stole down to the empty chamber at the end of the passageway.

But just as he padded by, the door swung open.

Will froze, praying he'd blend in with the shadows. As long as whoever it was didn't look his way—

"What are you doing roaming the corridor?" Percy's voice stabbed him in the back.

He turned, heart pounding—then angled his head. Why the deuce would his cousin be dressed head to toe in black, from the tips of his shoes, to his overcoat, to the dark hat clapped atop his head? "I could ask the same of you, Cousin. By the looks of it, you're in deep mourning and are about to go out to haunt the night."

Percy scowled. "Isn't your room there?" He lifted a finger and pointed back toward the blue room. "Why are you going in the opposite direction of your chamber?"

He stared down his nose, challenging Percy with a glower. "Just stretching my legs."

"As am I."

Will narrowed his eyes. Should he call the man on it? Clearly his cousin was up to no good. . .but then again, neither was he. He swept out his hand and gave Percy a little bow. "Enjoy your walk then."

"You as well." The sentiment was completely devoid of warmth, and in fact shivered in the space between them.

Percy turned, defiance hanging as thick and dark in the air as the shadows. Which one of them would discover the other's business first?

Chapter Twenty-Four

The beating of my heart was so violent and wild
that I felt as if my life were breaking from me.
Bleak House

Some days were the stuff made of dreams. This had been one, despite the slight shadow that it seemed Uncle Barlow purposely avoided a private conversation with either her or Will. But even so, Mina had still relished her morning stroll outside in an enchanted world of snow, dazzling like a thousand candlelit crystals. The afternoon was equally as magical, spent in a library nook in a greatly overstuffed chair with the time to untether her imagination. And most especially enthralling was catching the man she loved in the act of gazing at her when he thought she wasn't looking.

Mina hid a smile, but she couldn't conceal the pink that surely coloured her heated cheeks. Though Will stood on the other side of the drawing room in conversation with Percy, he always seemed to be aware of her—and that was the best dream of all.

On the settee, Uncle Barlow entertained Miss Whymsy with a botanical book and a magnifying glass—or did Miss Whymsy entertain him? Hard to tell, judging by the way their heads bowed together, sharing a secret laugh. Ahh, but this was a good respite for her older friend, for Mina suspected Miss Whymsy labored far too hard at the institute. The woman never did things by half measure.

Alice played a haunting tune on the piano, the last minor chords hovering on the air like an omen. Then she looked up and pinned Mina in place with the lift of her brow. "Mina, do come over here, would you? I think I've provided my fair portion of music for the evening. It is only right you share your talents, for I wouldn't dream of overshadowing your abilities."

She froze. The only thing she knew how to play was a short hand of whist, and even at that, her card skills were lacking. But music? Despite the many times she'd begged her father for lessons, there'd never been time or money. "I am sorry," she paused, searching for the right combination of words. "But I. . .I haven't played in years."

Immediately she bit the inside of her cheek. Was it a lie if she'd honestly not played in *any* of her years?

"A shame. I suppose William hasn't been able to afford a proper pianoforte for you. Even so, I have a remedy." Shuffling through papers, Alice pulled one out and held it up. "Ahh, here it is. I shall play, and you shall sing."

"Oh, I don't know. . ."

Uncle Barlow set down his magnifying glass and closed the book. "There's no need for such modesty here. Amongst friends, one should be able to share anything, especially one's voice."

Had ever a fox in a trap felt so ensnared? There was no possible way to get out of this short of feigning a sudden death.

Straightening her shoulders, she desperately hoped to find courage in good posture, then crossed over to Alice. Unless the woman had chosen a hymn or a pub song, it wasn't likely she'd be able to sing a word. She stopped at the end of the piano as the first chords rang out, each one unfamiliar. The expectancy in Uncle Barlow's eyes gleamed brilliant. Her corset bit into her ribs as she tried to control her frantic breathing. How to salvage this farce? *Think. Think!*

But nothing came to mind, least of all any lyrics. And why should they? She'd only read of ladies and high society. She surely didn't know what they'd sing, which only served to drive home the fact that no matter how much she'd like to, she didn't belong here.

Sneaking a glance over her shoulder, she eyed Alice, and a niggling thought crept out like a spider. . .did she *really* want to belong here, or would it turn her into a callous, hurtful woman such as Will's cousin? Apparently wealth alone didn't guarantee her life would have any more meaning than Alice's spiteful existence. Why had she wasted so many years thinking otherwise?

The music ground to a halt, pulling her from her thoughts, and she snapped her gaze to the floor, preferring to study the hem of her skirt rather than witness the disappointment in Uncle Barlow's eyes.

"That was your cue, Mina." Alice taunted from the keyboard. "Yet no matter. I'll begin again."

Unbearable heat churned up from her belly, and humiliation choked her. Suddenly she was eight years old again, standing amidst a circle of girls. Several pointing. Some laughing. All listening to the awful Mary Blake poke fun at her for being the daughter of a lunatic. Tears filled her eyes, blurring the world.

"How about something more seasonal? Alice, do you mind?"

She looked up to see Will wink at her as he strode to the piano keys. He forced Alice to yield the bench by his stare alone. Gently at first, then with more gusto, the opening chords of "God Rest Ye Merry, Gentlemen" filled the room like a gathering of old friends. This she could sing, and her knees weakened when Will joined in, his bass voice adding harmony. Even Uncle Barlow and Miss Whymsy sang along.

By the time the last note faded, Alice frowned. "That was quaint." She looped her arm through Mina's and pulled her away from the piano. "But I am tired of music. Let us take a turn about the room."

Unable to escape, Mina padded beside the tall woman, tongue lying fallow, heart fluttering. Why the sudden attention from Alice? Though she tried, she couldn't shake the feeling that this woman was a tiger hiding in the weeds, waiting to spring.

Alice didn't speak until they passed out of ear range of where Percy had once again cornered Will. "So, Mina, you don't sing the classics. You don't play. Where did you say you were educated?"

"I didn't." She let out a breath. That had been an easy answer.

"You didn't say, or you didn't have an education? Which is it?"

"I didn't say."

"Hmm." Alice eyed her sideways, her powdered face flawless in the sconce light. Maddeningly so. Except for the woman's cruel disposition, Alice overshadowed her in every way. "Where did you and William meet? Who introduced you? Perhaps I know the person."

She forced her arm to remain steady where it touched against Alice's, though surely if God struck her down for lying, her stillness would be in vain. "We met at. . .an establishment, and I doubt very much if you'd know any of our acquaintances."

"An establishment?" Alice pecked at the word like a vulture looking for the tastiest bits of meat. "Interesting. How long did you say you've been married?"

La! What was it Will had told her? A year? Nine months? Though she tried to recall what they'd worked out, the way Alice stared at her obliterated all her thoughts. "I. . .em. . ."

"Let me guess, you didn't say that either. I wonder if you can. A nondescript past, a nebulous engagement, and a mysterious marriage. That is more than intriguing." Alice stopped and turned, folding her hands in front of her as if they chatted about nothing more than ribbon colours or button sizes. "I find it interesting that a young woman so clearly in love hasn't much to say about her courtship or her husband. . .unless of course, he is *not* her husband."

Cold dread washed over her. Alice knew? How in the world? Or was the woman simply fishing for a scandal? Either way, the best option—the *only* option—was to exit as soon as possible. Mina threw back her shoulders, hoping such a regal pose would put Alice off—leastwise for now. "This turn of conversation is absurd. I am feeling tired, and I should like to retire now. Good night, Alice. I will see you on the morrow."

"Good night. Oh, and I won't bother sending William up after you, for I don't suppose it will matter what time he frequents the empty chamber at the end of the corridor, hmm?" Half a smile lifted the woman's lips, but it had nothing to do with mirth or amusement. "Though I must admit I am unsure if I should pity or scorn you for being such a naive little girl. At least Elizabeth knew what she'd been doing when her and Will had been together."

Mina whirled, praying the movement wouldn't be as panicky on the outside as the turmoil churning inside her. Forcing an impossible calmness to her steps, she strode toward the door—fighting the urge to bolt.

But as soon as she cleared the threshold, she raced to the stairs, and tears turned the world into a smear.

Oh, how she longed to go home.

CHAPTER TWENTY-FIVE

*Lies is lies. Howsever they come, they didn't ought to come,
and they come from the father of lies,
and work round to the same.*
Great Expectations

Will kept one eye trained on Mina while she strolled arm in arm with Alice, all the while listening to Percy blather on about the merits of steam engines. Something wasn't right about Alice's focused attention on Mina—and something was definitely wrong in the way Mina strode to the door with clipped steps and disappeared without a good night to anyone.

"Excuse me." He held up a hand to Percy, cutting him off. "It's been a long day. I bid you good night."

"Oh? Do you need a good leg stretcher tonight as well?"

"I could ask the same the same of you, Cousin. Any more clandestine meetings to attend?"

A tic pinched the skin at the corner of Percy's right eye. "Keep your nose out of my business, and perhaps I shall return the favor."

Will wheeled about, tired of Percy's games—and even wearier of his own.

"That's it. Run off to your cold bed in the spare room."

Percy's retort stabbed him in the back as he dashed out the door. How like his cousin to hold his cards close to his chest and pull one out at the most inopportune moment. Hopefully Uncle hadn't overheard.

But he'd have to deal with that later. For now, the way Mina flew up the stairway concerned him most. What horrid thing had Alice said to her?

"Mina, wait." He took the stairs two at a time.

She turned at the landing, face impossibly pale. Eyes so wide, she looked as if she'd not only seen a ghost, but held hands with one.

On impulse, he reached out and rubbed his hands along her upper arms, hoping to soothe. "What has you in such a state? What did Alice say to you?"

"She knows, Will." A little sob punctuated her words. "At least she suspects. And if your Uncle hears it from her—"

"Knows what?"

"That we are unwed."

He shook his head. "She can't possibly know that, not for certain. Please, Mina, don't fret. All will be well. This shall soon be over, I promise."

"I—" Her voice cracked. "I know."

Huge tears welled in her eyes, brimming like raindrops and shimmering in the lamplight. His heart twisted at the sight. Grabbing her hand, he led her away from the landing and into the corridor, out of view should anyone chance to leave the drawing room.

He turned to her well before they reached her chamber door, unwilling to spend another second without easing the burden that drove her to weep. Reaching out, he cupped her face, catching her tears before they dampened her cheeks. "Tell me true, Mina. What is wrong? Did I not say this would soon be over?"

"That's just it! This will *all* be over soon. And then what? We go back to being what we were, me serving you ale once a week while you and Mr. Fitzroy swap jokes?" She threw out her hands, the passion in her eyes far too alluring. "Is any of this even real?"

"It is." Without thinking, he bent, and his mouth came down on hers. The heat of a thousand suns burned along every nerve and settled low in his belly. Everything went oddly quiet. The hiss of the gas lamps. The beat of his heart. There was nothing else but Mina's sweet taste. Her breath. Her softness. A tremor shook through him, and he hungered for more. Every other kiss in his life had been wrong. He knew that now—and would never again kiss another.

"Mina," he whispered against her lips, her jawline, her neck. Lost. Hopelessly, wonderfully lost.

A low moan sounded in her throat, sobering him. What was he doing? He pulled back.

Mina's eyes were yet closed, lashes impossibly long against her cheeks. She lifted a shaky finger to her lips and absently rubbed a mouth yet swollen with his kisses. Was she remembering—or abhorring?

He sucked in a breath. "Forgive me. I shouldn't have taken such a liberty. I don't usually—"

Her eyes popped open, and an unnatural brilliance shone in them. . .a fevered kind of fury.

"Don't you? Did you kiss Elizabeth like that as well?" she hissed.

The question slapped him in the face—hard—and he recoiled a step. "How do you know of her?"

"Your cousins have mentioned her several times." The red glints in her hair matched the colour rising in her cheeks. "Was she another one of your pretend brides?"

He spun away as if struck, tensing every muscle in his body. "No," he gritted out. "She was to be my real bride." The truth hung thick between them.

"I've heard enough. Good night, William."

"Mina, wait!" He pivoted back. "I can explain. Let me explain."

"No. I'm done with your explanations. I can't do this anymore. I can't." Her voice shook. "The twisted truths. The deceit. I. . ." She shook her head, knocking loose a single curl. "I will be leaving in the morning."

"Mina, don't do this." The thought of losing her drove the breath from his lungs. He was as thoroughly sick of deception as she, but dare he voice the truth he could no longer deny? "I. . ." Swallowing, he reached for her and pulled her close. "I love you, Mina. With all my heart."

She stiffened beneath his touch. Blinking. Face the colour of parchment. "I wish I could believe that. I really do." Her voice was a shiver of cold wind. "But I meant what I said. I am leaving in the morning."

Wrenching from his grasp, she whirled, the hem of her skirt snapping against his legs.

"Mina!"

He followed her frenzied pace, but too late. She reached her chamber door and slammed it in his face before he could catch her, the slide of the bolt overloud as it shot into place. He stood alone in the corridor with naught but the echo and far too many regrets.

CHAPTER TWENTY-SIX

A dream, all a dream, that ends in nothing,
and leaves the sleeper where he lay down.
A Tale of Two Cities

Lethargic light, a sickly sort of blue-grey, leached through the open drapery like a spreading bruise. Clutching the second-chance coin, Mina shoved off the bed, fully dressed, more wrinkled than the counterpane she'd wrestled with all night. Weary to the very marrow of her bones, she paced to the window and pressed her forehead against the glass. The coldness of it shocked and jarred—and she welcomed the bite.

"I love you, Mina. With all my heart."

Will's words of the night before haunted relentlessly, and she squeezed the coin all the tighter. Did he *really* mean it, or was it his desperate attempt to get her to stay? She'd give anything to believe his love was true, but though she tried, she just couldn't. The coin pressed hard into her skin. She could give him another chance to explain about Elizabeth, but even if she did, how would she know for sure he spoke truth?

She blew out a breath, fogging a clouded circle on the window. Mostly she just wanted to go home. She missed Father's bellowing and Cook's mumblings of "peas and porridge." Life at the Golden Egg was a lackluster existence compared to the eminence and elegance of this country estate, but it was her existence. And more importantly, it was real. Not a charade. Without truth as a base, even living the lifestyle of the wealthy didn't give her life meaning.

Maybe—perhaps—true meaning in life had nothing to do with outward trappings but with inward genuineness.

A foreign longing welled to run back to the inn and embrace her dull life. She was done with pretending. And done with casting Will as a hero, for he had been a dream. A fleeting, make-believe man she'd invented—and who'd fallen woefully short. She'd love to blame him, to rage and rail against his shortcomings, but truly, was she not as culpable for expecting more out of him than was humanly possible?

Oh, God. I have been so wrong. Please, forgive me.

Outside, an ember of sun lit the charcoal sky. Across the courtyard, the door to the stables opened, and a young man strolled out, dressed for the day's work of tending horses. Good. Then it wouldn't be too soon to request a ride into town.

Turning from the sight, she hurried over to the dressing table and sank onto the stool. There wasn't much she could do about her wrinkled gown, but she ought to at least see to her hair, especially with a full day of travel ahead.

As she wrangled out snarls, she studied her face in the mirror. Her eyes were too big. Her nose, overly long and dotted with freckles. Her lips were too full and remembered far too well the feel of Will's mouth fitted against them. The hairbrush slipped from her grasp, and she caught it before it hit the carpet. No, not again. She'd spent the entire night trying to forget that kiss.

And failed.

She cast the brush onto the table and poked pins into her hair, grazing her scalp. Had Will spoken the same words of love to Elizabeth? Had Elizabeth been as naive as she to wish they were true?

No more. She shoved up from the table and retrieved her coat, tucking the second-chance coin into the pocket. It was too early to trouble Miss Whymsy's door, but perhaps by the time she finished talking with the stable hand, the older lady would be stirring.

The corridors were yet dim, and she tread as quickly as she dared without bumping into a side table or tripping down the stairway. She paused in the foyer, debating if she ought to use the front door. But no, better to use the back servants' entrance, for that's what she really was despite her pretending otherwise.

Outside, cold air violated the hem of her skirts and climbed up her legs. It wasn't far from the house to the stables, but by the time she ducked inside to the smell of hay and horses, she wished she had thought to grab her muffler.

The same young man she'd seen earlier turned from a workbench at her entrance and dipped his head. "Can I be of service to ye, ma'am?"

"Yes. I was wondering if you could bring around the carriage and drive my traveling companion and me to Bishop's Stortford. We shall be catching the morning train to London."

"Aye, ma'am. I'll bring it 'round within the hour."

"Thank you." Clutching her coat tighter at the neck, she headed back out into the nip of the winter morning. Hopefully Miss Whymsy was up, though it was a shameful task to have to ask her friend to leave so soon after convincing her to come in the first place. In the four days they'd been here, the woman had seemed to enjoy herself, especially when Uncle Barlow was in the room.

Halfway across the courtyard, she paused, wishing to brand into her memory the elegance of the white-stone estate. Would she ever have another chance to Christmas in the country? It had been lovely—while it lasted. Sighing, she swept her gaze from the snow-crusted windowsills of the ground level, up to the first floor, then paused on the nearest window on the second. The drapes were pulled back and a face stared out, framed with white, tufted hair.

She gasped. Why was Uncle Barlow frowning at her? Had Alice already gone to him with her suspicions? Her shoulders slumped as she imagined his disappointment. Good thing she'd arranged for transport, for surely Will's uncle would be asking her to leave within the hour.

With a half-hearted wave at the face in the window, she continued toward the house—but he kept staring at a point beyond her. Had he never really been looking at her to begin with? She turned, then squinted for a better look.

On the side of the road leading into town, two dark shapes stood in conversation near a horse swishing its tail. One man wore glasses—easy enough to identify as Percy. The other was a rotund fellow, nearly twice the breadth of Percy, and wearing a ridiculously tall hat. Did he think that made him appear any less roly-poly than the great ball of black wool that he was? An odd time for a conversation and an even odder place in which to conduct their business.

But it was no business of hers. Not anymore. She ducked her head into the cold breeze and pressed on toward the house. It was time to rouse Miss Whymsy—and leave all this behind.

Chapter Twenty-Seven

*If our affections be tried, our affections are our consolation
and comfort; and memory, however sad, is the best
and purest link between this world and a better.*
Nicholas Nickleby

Will descended the stairs two at a time. Was he too late? Was Mina already now on her way back to London?

His foot landed crooked on a step, and he grabbed for the balustrade. Falling headlong would slow his pursuit—but not end it. If he had to run through the snow all the way to the Golden Egg, he would explain the full truth to Mina. He owed her that. He owed himself that. And most importantly, he owed it to God.

Both his feet landed on the foyer floor, and the sound of swishing skirts turned him. With one hand yet on the railing, he memorized Mina's graceful shape—for she'd likely never want to see him again after this. "Thank God you're still here," he spoke more to the heavens than to her.

"Not for long." She stopped at the foot of the stairs and lifted her chin. "Goodbye, Will."

Her words were cold. Final. Like nails being hammered into a coffin.

He reached out and grabbed her arm, gently yet firmly. "Mina, listen, just for a moment, and then you may be on your way."

She stared at his fingers on her sleeve. "There can be nothing more to say. You will not talk me out of leaving."

"I don't intend to. I simply want to explain about Elizabeth.

That's all. I swear it."

Pulling from his touch, she met his gaze, her blue eyes a sword, seeking to cleave away any more lies. "You don't owe me an explanation. It is your uncle you should be talking to."

"I know. And I will." He plowed his fingers through his hair, the movement as wild as the beat of his heart. "But a word with you first, please."

With a sigh, she leaned her back against the stair rail, resignation bending her brow. "What is it you have to say?"

He widened his stance, for speaking the past aloud was sure to knock him sideways. Just thinking of it put him off-balance. "Though I hate to admit it, in my younger years, I lived solely for wine, women, and making merry. It was then I met Elizabeth Hill, at a house party, for much to my shame, *I* was the life of the party."

His head drooped, and he studied his shoes. Memories twisted his gut. Too much drink. Too many indiscretions. Unknowingly, he'd lived the same debauched life as his father before him.

"You don't have to tell me this," Mina murmured.

"No, I. . ." He jerked his face back to hers. If he didn't get this out now, he never would. "Even then Uncle was gracious, urging me to stop the ribald lifestyle and settle down. I thought taking a wife who enjoyed a good time as much as I might be a way to pacify him while continuing to live unbridled; for you see, Elizabeth loved her social life as much as I did mine. She was agreeable to my proposal, and I even fancied myself in love with her."

Mina's jaw clenched, the fine lines of her throat hardening to steel. "The very words you spoke to me last night."

He drew a deep breath, willing the truth he'd known all along to finally pass his lips. "No. It's not the same at all. You have taught me that there's a great deal of difference between self-love and self-sacrificing love. You didn't have to come here. You didn't have to help me try to save Uncle Barlow, yet you did so, willingly. Elizabeth never would have done such a thing unless she had something to gain for herself."

Mina bit her lip, her teeth worrying the flesh, almost in time to the corridor clock ticking away.

And Will prayed, pleading for truth to win, for past sins to be forgotten. For Mina to give him a second chance.

Stepping away from her post at the railing, she paced a small figure on the rug, and a quick slice of fear cut through him from head to toe. Did she mean to run off now? To turn her back to him as Elizabeth had?

But she stopped, inches from him, her face unreadable. "What happened to her? To Elizabeth, for you said she was to be your bride, not that she *was* your bride."

It wasn't much, but the barest flicker in Mina's eyes birthed a hope in him. Maybe—perhaps—she actually would hear him out and come to believe his feelings for her were true. *Oh, God, make it so.*

"Elizabeth broke off the engagement," he began, "for she'd worked her way into the graces of an earl. I don't blame her—now, that is. I did then. That was a black period. An angry one."

Ghosts of the past curled about him like thick smoke, and he tugged at his collar. "My bitterness drove me to worse sins, chief amongst them gaming. Were it not for Uncle Barlow, I'd still be wallowing in debtor's prison."

Her eyes narrowed. "What do you mean?"

"Uncle Barlow paid all that I owed—and more. He arranged for me to be taken on as a law clerk. God knows I didn't deserve that kind of mercy, and I couldn't understand why he did such a thing. Yet for his sake, I tried to live in a more respectable manner. Shortly thereafter, Fitz invited me to a church service, and then I knew. Funny, is it not, that one doesn't know how bad one really is until trying hard to be good."

Pausing, he revisited that holy day. The sacred union. The wonder of it even now was enough to pump warmth through his veins.

A small smile twitched his lips. "Uncle's extravagant act of compassion paled in comparison to the grace God offered me that day. I've never been the same. Oh, how that must sound coming from my mouth. For you know better than most that I am not a saint."

Small, white fingers appeared on his sleeve, and she pressed hope into his arm with a little squeeze. "Thank you for telling me."

A lump clogged his throat and he fought to clear it. "I've been such a fool. I should have left Uncle's well-being to God instead of taking it on myself." Collecting her hand in his, he dropped to one knee and tipped up his face. "I don't deserve it, but will you forgive me, Mina, for pulling you into this deceitful plan of mine?"

Slowly, she nodded. "Of course, but I am still leaving."

"I wouldn't dream of stopping you—"

"A very pretty time to propose now." Footsteps thudded on the floor as Percy rounded the other side of the stairs and stopped in front of them. A smile spread across his face like gangrene, sick and deadly.

Will shot to his feet, but before he could utter a word of defense, Percy continued, "I wonder what Uncle will say when he discovers your deceit?"

He threw out his hands. It was either that or throttle the man. "I am not propos—"

"What is this?" Uncle Barlow's voice shook from above, and they all pivoted to see him descending the stairs.

"These two are a fraud, Uncle Barlow." With a fierce sweep of his hand, Percy aimed his finger at him and Mina, casting them both into destruction. "William and Mina are not married."

Uncle Barlow's footsteps fell heavy on the stairs, and he looked down upon them as God himself. "I know."

Chapter Twenty-Eight

To conceal anything from those to whom I am attached
is not in my nature. I can never close my lips
where I have opened my heart.
Master Humphrey's Clock

Uncle Barlow's revelation echoed from wall to wall, hanging a pall in the air, thick as cream, and smothering the breath from Mina's lungs. *He knew?* She didn't dare look at Will. The devastation on his face would surely match hers, and it was hard enough to maintain her own composure without having to witness his.

Uncle Barlow descended the last stair, his feet landing on the foyer's tiled floor like a crack of thunder. He stood there for a moment, saying nothing, staring at each one in turn, the disappointment in his eyes nearly driving her to her knees.

"I would have a word with all of you. In my study." He turned and strode off, his steps echoing in the stunned silence left behind.

Percy flashed them a wicked smile, then immediately fell into step behind Uncle Barlow. And no wonder he was so eager, for he renewed his tirade slandering her and Will, devoting them to ruin as they trailed him. Percy's words were awful—because they were true. Oh, that she'd never gone along with this scheme to begin with. Her step faltered, and Will reached for her hand.

They entered a wood-paneled room with books lining two of the walls. Directly behind a desk at center, Uncle Barlow sat as judge and jury. Will led her to stand in front of the desk, with him as a buffer between her and Percy. But that left nothing between her and the snarling head of a skinned tiger, lying inches from her feet. The flattened carcass made for a fine rug except for its head, which had been left intact. The fangs gleamed ivory and sharp at the pointed ends, and at the roots nearest the lips, darkened to a brownish, dried-blood colour. How much flesh had those teeth torn into?

"I demand you cast these two sinners out into the cold." Percy's voice snarled, and she jerked her gaze away from the dead danger to the one very much alive. "William has besmirched the Barlow name by taking a woman who's not legally his wife."

"I have not!" Will splayed his fingers, dropping her hand and daring a step closer to his Uncle's desk. "Mina's virtue is—and never has been—violated. She is innocent, and I take full blame for the deceit in which I convinced her to partake."

Percy tipped his chin to a pert angle. "One cannot believe the words of a deceiver."

Will spun toward him, jaw clenched so tightly a muscle stood out like a rod on his neck. "Nor can one believe the tales of a schemer."

"Enough!" Uncle Barlow's voice bellowed sharp and black, absorbing all light and air and objections.

Caught between the fangs of the tiger and the three man-beasts roaring in a fury, Mina edged back a step.

Uncle Barlow swung his gaze to Percy. "I also know of your devious plans, Percival. I have had my suspicions all along. Your clandestine meeting this morning with Mr. Greaves merely confirmed them. Very sloppy of you to meet in view of the house."

"Don't be ridiculous! There was nothing clandestine about it."

From this angle, slightly behind Percy and off to the side a bit, the morning light leaching in through the windows outlined his frame—and it shook slightly.

So did Percy's voice. "Fallon Greaves and I go way back. I was merely passing on the prospect of having him join in my investment venture. Nothing more."

Uncle Barlow leaned aside and opened a top drawer, and as he rifled through papers, Will leaned aside as well, whispering for her alone, "Mr. Greaves is the administrator of the Bishop's Stortford Asylum."

"You mean—?"

Her whisper was cut off by the sharp slap of a document landing on the desktop and the stab of Uncle Barlow's finger skewering it in place. "Are you speaking of this venture, Percy?"

In two long strides, Percy snatched the paper from off the desk. The parchment quivered in his grasp as his gaze swept over it. "Where did you get this?"

"Do you really think me senile?" Uncle Barlow leaned back in his chair and folded his arms. "That night at dinner, when you shoved document after document in my face, I took the liberty of memorizing several names. I contacted them, which led me to other names, and eventually on to a devolving list of men who are none too pleased with you at the moment. Apparently you've pledged more investment dollars than you've paid. In short, you are in debt to some very powerful men."

For once, Percy said nothing, though his mouth opened and closed several times like a landed halibut.

"Uncle Barlow," Will broke the awful silence. "My intent was to protect you from Percy's schemes. Please allow me to explain."

The older man shot up his hand, shoving William's words right back at him. "No explanation needed. I have known since you arrived that you were not married. But there is one thing I do not know." Will's uncle turned his grey gaze to her. "Tell me, Miss Scott, what is it you hoped to gain by going along with my misguided nephew and this ridiculous farce? What did he promise you?"

Her corset cut into her ribs. Breathing was out of the question. It would be better to stare at the tiger's fangs than to stand in the glare of such righteous damnation. But she couldn't look away from the furious disappointment glowering out from Uncle Barlow's soul—for she deserved it.

"Nothing, sir." The words squeaked out impossibly small, and she tried again. "I stood to gain nothing at all, save for the chance to hopefully prevent you from being forced into an existence no one should have to suffer. There is nothing but death in an asylum, and I know of what I speak, for my mother suffered such a fate. After discovering Percy's true intent, I couldn't let that happen to you. Yet I confess Will and I went about it the wrong way. It was wrong of me to have deceived you, and for that I am woefully sorry. I can do nothing but beg for your forgiveness."

Tears burned her eyes, for something precious had been lost. Not since her grandfather had she shared so thoroughly her love of literature—not even with Miss Whymsy. Would that Uncle Barlow were in possession of the second-chance coin instead of her.

On the other side of Will, Percy started clapping, the sharp ring of his hands echoing from wall to wall. "Stunning performance, Miss Scott. Where did you say you picked this one up, Will—on Drury Lane, was it?"

"Leave off!" Will moved so fast, air whooshed against her cheek. He grabbed Percy up by the lapels, twisting the fabric until wheezes garbled in Percy's throat. "You are finished disparaging Mina."

Uncle Barlow shook his head, clearly disgusted. "Let go of your cousin, William. Violence solves nothing."

Will let go—but not without a little shove. "Leave Mina out of this, Cousin." Then he turned to his uncle. "I take complete responsibility for having persuaded Mina to act as my wife. It was wrong. *I* was wrong. Do not blame her."

Will's defense wrapped around her as warm as an embrace.

Percy tugged at the hems of his sleeves, straightening each one. "On the contrary, the woman is every bit as deceitful as my cousin—on par with Will's mother. . .for she is alive. Alive and well and living in France. No doubt packing her bags even this minute in hopes of setting up house here." He spread his arms.

Next to her, Will stiffened.

Uncle Barlow jerked as if he'd been struck. "Is this true, William?"

Mina stared, horrified, at Will. What would he say? Would he deny it or tell all?

His head dropped. His shoulders. Even the very air around him seemed to deflate. "It is true, sir. My mother is alive. But I swear I did not know it until only recently, and she made me vow to—"

"Stop. I've heard enough." Uncle Barlow scrubbed a hand over his face. Again and again. "I think it best that you all leave— and not just this study, but my home. I withdraw my Christmas invitation."

"But Uncle, surely you're not going to listen to a word of such drivel spoken by a liar and a loose skirt." Percy's voice tightened until it cracked. "William is not fit to inherit."

Uncle Barlow shot to his feet and slammed his fists on the desktop. "Neither of you are. Now out!"

Percy whirled, muttering oaths and calling down brimstone upon them all.

Will reached for her hand. "Let us leave, Mina."

She lagged behind, her heart laying in pieces somewhere on the floor back near the tiger's mouth. How abominable this whole thing had turned out. . .and not just for her, but most especially for Will. Lord knows he didn't deserve it, but would Uncle Barlow consider giving him yet another chance? It would take a miracle, an act of God—yet was that not what

Christmas-time was really all about?

Wrenching from Will's grasp, she turned back and marched to Uncle Barlow's desk. She shoved her hand into her pocket and pulled out the second-chance coin, worn now like a talisman, and set it down on the desk.

Uncle Barlow glowered. "You cannot buy back my good opinion, Miss Scott, and in fact, have only worsened it in the attempt to do so."

"I—I would never think of it, sir. I will only say this. A friend of mine gave me this coin, but I think, perhaps, you have greater need of it than I."

He said nothing, and behind her, William's whisper travelled from the door, "Mina, come along."

But if she didn't say these words now, she'd never get another chance. She pointed at the coin. "That small piece of gold is a second-chance coin. I've kept it, wondering who to give it to, and now I know. I give it to you and plead that you'll see fit to give William a second chance—again. He's told me of his past, and I don't blame you for thinking ill of him. Yet the man I know now is not the same as the man that he was. He did change after you redeemed him from gaol."

Uncle Barlow's grey eyes hardened to steel. "You will forgive me if I favor the evidence I've seen rather than your word."

"Evidence that is incomplete, for the full truth is that William's mother is sick, and she made him promise not to alert you. He's been using his own funds to pay for her doctor fees and apothecary bills. Her room and board. Will didn't wish to get you out of the way in order to spend your money, like Percy did. He merely hoped to use the collateral of the inheritance to gain a small loan from a banker to continue her care. It had nothing to do with wealth or greed but to hopefully save the life of another human being. As misdirected as it was, Will acted out of love and kindness, nothing more. I will be the first to admit he is a flawed man, but he is a good one, and I hope you can find it in your heart to forgive him."

Without waiting for a rebuttal—for she'd spent all she'd had to say anyway—Mina turned and strode out the study door.

Past a gaping William.

Chapter Twenty-Nine

There ain't a gent'lman in all the land—
nor yet sailing upon all the sea—
that can love his lady more than I love her.
David Copperfield

After a last glance over his shoulder at his uncle's estate, Will descended the final stair and dashed to catch up to the carriage setting off down the lane. The cold tried to nip him, but a white-hot sense of failure burned within. He'd likely never see Uncle Barlow again, and for that he was truly sorry.

"Hold up!" He shouted to the driver.

The man pulled back on the reins with a "Whoa."

Slipping on the snow, Will flung out his arms to keep from tumbling, then slid-walked the rest of the way to the carriage door. It would be a long trek to town should Mina and Miss Whymsy deny his request to board. But even if they consented, the ride would likely be just as long. The humiliation Mina had suffered on his account had been no small matter. He wouldn't blame her if she gave him an earful, or worse—icy silence.

He opened the door and hefted himself up onto the step, sticking only his head inside. Miss Whymsy blinked at him from one seat, Mina from the other.

"I know I'm likely the last person either of you ladies would want to share a carriage with, but my cousins have taken the other coach, and the horse I rode here is lame. May I ride with you into town?"

Miss Whymsy frowned. "You'll catch your death out there. Of course you may ride with us. Come in."

"Thank you." He yanked the door shut and latched it, then jockeyed for the best place to sit. The older lady sat on one seat with a large bag next to her, overflowing with books. He could squeeze between the bag and wall—maybe. It would be a tight fit.

But Mina gathered her skirts and shifted to make room for him. The carriage heaved into motion, and he sat before he fell upon either of them.

The wheels crunched through the snow. Horses' snorts added to the jingle of tack and harness. He turned to Mina, and she to him, but words stuck sharp in his throat. How was he to tell her how sorry he was? How proud he'd been when she'd defended him to Uncle? How he hoped she could somehow forgive him? Regret upon regret heaped into a great pile and sank in his gut. He'd laughed off many things in his life, but here, now, staring into the endless fathoms of Mina's blue eyes, he doubted he'd ever smile again.

Across from them, Miss Whymsy clucked her tongue. "It's rather hard to breathe, what with the elephant taking up so much space in here."

They both turned their heads toward the woman, Mina giving hers a little shake. "What elephant, Miss Whymsy?"

"Posh! I may be old, child, but I'm not blind. There is clearly much on both of your minds." Leaning sideways, she pulled out a thick book from her bag and shook it at them. "I shall be otherwise occupied, so have at it."

She plopped the book onto her lap and opened it with one gloved finger, ignoring them.

The woman was right. He had far too much on his mind, but what to say? Where to begin? He blew out a long breath, creating a frosty little cloud, then turned back to Mina.

"Mina—"

"Will—"

Her name blended with his on the air, and she shrank back.

"No, no." He shook his head. "Ladies first. I would hear what you have to say. All of it. No matter what."

Bracing himself for the onslaught, perhaps even tears, he clenched the seat so hard his knuckles cracked.

But a strange transformation took place. Mina's face softened beneath the brim of her bonnet. Her brows knit, not in an angry twist, but slanted with a bend of compassion. "Oh, Will, I am sorry for the way things turned out. I know money will be a stretch for you, what with your mother's illness. But one thing I've learned from all this is that there are more important things than wealth. Spending time with your cousins showed me that pretty dresses and dining in fine establishments doesn't necessarily bring significance. Significance comes in caring—really caring—for those around us. Please don't misunderstand, I know you do care for your uncle, and I'm not for one minute saying you don't, but you—I—went about it in the wrong way."

She paused, and the fine lines of her throat bobbed. "I can honestly say now that as mundane as my life is with Father, I would rather smile with him over a simple bowl of oyster stew on Christmas than to sit at one more linen-clothed table with Percy or Alice. There's value in that, in the sharing of joy and tears, and that's what makes life worthwhile. Not what we do or what we accomplish. I have you to thank for that revelation, for had you never asked me to be your pretend bride, I'd still be wishing to be someone or somewhere else."

His chest tightened, and breathing turned into a chore. Had ever a more gracious woman lived? She should've railed at him. Cursed him. Blamed him for the beastly way she'd been treated by his cousins...and by him, for he was the one who'd dragged her into this situation.

"I know you're disappointed with how things turned out, but at the very least—" A small smile curved her lips. "Your uncle won't be committed to an asylum. And that's what we were working toward all along. It was a hard victory, but a victory nonetheless."

"And for that I am thankful." He attempted to match her smile, but bitter remorse stole his last reserves of humour, and he could do no better than manage somewhat of a grimace. "I regret, however, that I've broken the very thing I'd hoped to mend, namely my relationship with Uncle Barlow. I doubt he will ever speak to me again. Nor should he."

A ray of sunshine broke through the clouds, angling in through the window and resting upon Mina as a halo. "But how could he remain angry with you? The truth of what you did, while draped in duplicity, was for the benefit of him, not yourself. You are a man of integrity, despite how sideways it comes out."

Her words and the admiration shining in her eyes did much to soothe his soul—but could do nothing to erase the stain of his past.

"You give me too much credit, Mina." And she did. God knew he was as big a schemer as his cousin. "If I'd been up front with Uncle to begin with, left everything in God's hands instead of taking the situation into my own, none of this would have happened."

She reached out and squeezed his hand. "I think we both learned a lesson, hmm?"

Without thinking, he covered her glove with his own, sandwiching her hand between his. How small, yet how strong. How would it feel to gather her in his arms and—

The carriage jolted and his leg bumped against hers. Red bloomed on her cheeks, and the thin space between them charged like the air before a lightning strike. He sucked in a breath. So did she. Their gazes met—and held.

"Oh, for heaven's sake." Miss Whymsy slammed her book shut. "Now would be the time, Mr. Barlow."

"The time for what?" he asked without shifting his gaze.

"Love is surely wasted on youth. There is no better time to ask

Miss Scott to marry you than now."

Choking on the suggestion, he released Mina's hand and brought his fist to his mouth to keep from spluttering.

Mina's jaw dropped—and a strange light of hope kindled in her eyes.

Lowering his hand, he tugged at his collar. Air. He needed air, and lots of it. As much as he wanted to make Mina his own, how could he possibly take on a wife and care for his mother on a law clerk's salary?

He slipped a sideways glance at the older lady. "You overstep, madam."

"I think not. Clearly the two of you are in love. Do you deny it?"

Heat burned a trail from his gut to his heart—especially when he shifted his gaze back to Mina.

"Your answer, Mr. Barlow?" Miss Whymsy prodded.

Gads! Had the woman been a lion tamer before she'd retired?

"No," he said, staring deep into Mina's eyes. "I do not deny it."

Mina lifted her chin. "Nor do I."

His breath hitched, and for a moment he dared imagine a future of love and life and joy. Of whispers in the dark of night and blue-eyed babies with copper-streaked hair.

But then the carriage wheels dipped into a rut, jolting him to reality. Love, no matter how pure, did not put food on the table or a roof overhead. "Mina, I—" his voice broke, and he swallowed. "I'm sorry. I have nothing to offer you. Once I move my mother here, I'll be sharing a one-room flat with her, and there will still be doctor bills to pay. I cannot ask you to endure such a hardship."

"Of course you can," she murmured.

He leaned closer. Surely he hadn't heard her right. "What?"

"You *can* ask me. One room or ten, it doesn't matter as long as you're in the room with me. I'm done with playing the part of a lady. I've had my tea at Purcell's. My dinner in a London townhouse. Even a holiday of sorts at a country estate. The only kind of lady I want to be is yours. Truly, that's all I've ever wanted from the minute you first asked me to be your pretend bride."

He gaped. "Do you mean that, knowing all you do about me?"

She beamed. "I do."

Was this real? Had she just agreed to be his wife? As the carriage wheels rattled along, so did a hundred more questions turn round and round in his head.

"For pity's sake, lad," Miss Whymsy scolded. "Kiss the woman!"

Oh, hang it all. Without a clue as to how he'd manage providing for a new wife and an ailing mother, he pulled Mina into his arms and kissed her soundly.

CHAPTER THIRTY

For it is good to be children sometimes,
and never better than at Christmas,
when its mighty Founder was a child himself.
A Christmas Carol

Snugging the bow tight on the small package, Mina lifted Father's gift for inspection as the mantel clock struck six. She jumped to her feet. No time to waste! Guests were likely already arriving, maybe even Will. The thought sent her heart tripping and her feet moving. She dashed over to her chamber door and slipped out.

She'd been right. Merry chatter and laughter wafted up the stairs from the taproom, the sound of "Happy Christmas!" being bantered about. The savory scent of oyster stew filled the entire inn. Upping her pace, she raced along the corridor to Father's room.

She rapped her knuckles against the wood and hid the gift behind her back with her other hand. "Father? It's time."

"Coming, girl."

The door swung open. Father stood with one hand behind his back, dressed in his finest grey serge suit. His hazel eyes twinkled. "I've got something for ye, daughter."

She grinned. "And I for you."

"Ye ready?" He fairly bounced on his toes, as giddy as a young lad.

Her grin grew. Ahh, but she'd miss this tradition, the private exchange of gifts between her and Father before celebrating with friends. Yet just because she would be married next Christmas, surely that didn't have to mean an end to all her traditions with

Father, and in fact, she determined, it would not.

"Ready." She met her father's gaze, and they counted down in unison. "Three. Two. One."

She held out her gift. So did Father—and they both tore into the wrappings, bits of paper flying and falling to the floor like snow.

"Oh, my girl. How thoughtful!" Emotion roughened his voice. "Ye could've bought a fob and yet ye took the time to make me one?" He yanked out his pocket watch and wound the braided twist through the loop. "It's perfect."

Forgetting her own gift, she grinned, wide and carefree. "I am happy you think so. I know Mother always intended to purchase you a gold chain, and I still hope to someday carry out that wish."

"No, child. This is dearer to me than a bit of shiny metal, especially now that ye'll be leaving me." He ran a gnarled knuckle along her cheek. "Now go on. Finish opening yours."

Pulling off the last of the brown wrapper, she sucked in a breath. "Oh, Father!" she whispered.

Fingers trembling, she flipped open the cover of a somewhat frayed copy of *David Copperfield* and caressed the title page. In all her twenty-three years, Father had never once given her a book, and she hugged it to her chest. "I shall cherish this always."

Father's big arms wrapped around her, and he pulled her close. "Just as I cherish you, my girl. Happy Christmas, now and always."

A sob caught in her throat, and she nuzzled her face against his waistcoat. As thrilled as she was to become Will's wife, she would be hesitant to leave her day-to-day life with this man. "Happy Christmas, Father," she murmured.

He gave her a little squeeze, then released her. "Our company awaits. Shall we?"

Sniffling back tears, she looped her arm through his and gave him a wavering smile. "We shall."

Her steps faltered only once as they descended the stairs—when the blue of William's eyes met hers from across the room.

But Father halted her two steps from the taproom floor, so that they looked out over the patrons filling the Golden Egg. A more merry sight she couldn't imagine. The room was draped with holly bunting. Strings of cranberries and nuts and raisins swagged back and forth across the ceiling. Everyone smiled and chattered, and best of all, Will shouldered his way through the crowd toward her, the gleam of love in his eyes stealing her breath.

"Friends!" Father bellowed.

All turned his way, and the din lowered to a muted hum.

"Welcome one and all to the annual Golden Egg Christmas Eve celebration, but before I serve what I know yer all waitin' on—"

"Bring out the stew! Bring out the stew!" The chant started low then grew in intensity.

Releasing his hold on her arm, Father lifted his hands. "Aye! Stew ye shall have. But first, an announcement. Mr. Barlow, if you wouldn't mind joining us."

With a grin and a wink, Will hopped up on the bottom stair and entwined his fingers with hers.

"It is with great pleasure that I should like to announce—"

Just then, the front door burst open, and along with a blast of chill air and a flurry of snowflakes, in bustled a surprising collection of new arrivals. Uncle Barlow's grey hair tufted out from the brim of his hat. Next to him was Miss Whymsy, who walked next to a tall lady with an assured step.

And behind them marched Percy and Alice.

"An announcement, you say?" Uncle Barlow doffed his hat. "Then we've arrived just in time. I should like to make an announcement."

Mina tensed, and Will's hand squeezed hers.

Father leaned close and whispered in her ear. "Who is that?"

"Will's uncle," she whispered back.

"Ahh. Fitting that his family join us." Straightening, Father motioned for the newcomers to work their way to the stairs. "Come,

come. We will do this together."

But she couldn't quite work up the same amount of excitement that boomed in Father's voice. What would Uncle Barlow say? Had he forgiven Will? Or her?

Will pulled her close. "Have faith, Mina. We've done all we could. Let us leave this in God's hands, as we should have from the start."

The crowd cleared a space for the entourage, and Uncle Barlow dipped his head toward Father. "Thank you, sir." Then he faced the crowd. "In this season of giving, there can be no better time than to announce to whom I shall give my estate. And so, tonight, amongst family and friends—"he beamed down at Miss Whymsy— "I should like to name the heir of the Barlow lands."

Percy and Alice leaned closer.

Miss Whymsy smiled broadly at the lady next to her.

Mina held her breath. *Please, God, have mercy.*

"I shall place my holdings in a trust, to be used exclusively for the Institute for the Care of Sick Gentlewomen, which is directed by my new friend here, Miss Florence Nightingale."

The lady next to Miss Whymsy clapped her hands with a, "Hear, hear!" that would've made Miss Minton proud.

The institute? But how had the old fellow. . .of course. Miss Whymsy must've spoken of it. Mina couldn't help but smile. What a perfectly fitting solution for Uncle Barlow and the institute.

"Yet," Uncle Barlow continued, "I shall need an administrator to live at the estate to manage the funding and all other details. A trustworthy administrator. One who knows the house and lands like none other, and who of course shall be well compensated."

Percy stepped forward.

But Uncle Barlow extended his hand toward Will; the old, worn, second-chance coin resting on his upturned palm. "What say you, my boy?"

Without letting go of her hand, Will reached for the coin with his other. "Only if I may bring my wife along."

Uncle Barlow's gaze swung toward her. "In truth?"

"Aye!" Father belted. "And that's my announcement. Lift yer mugs in toast and honor to the happy new couple. We make merry tonight, and in four weeks' time, shall make merry again with the marriage of my daughter to Mr. William Barlow."

A roar shook to the rafters, followed by a hearty, "Bring out the stew!"

Which prodded Father into action. He trotted down the last few stairs then disappeared into the kitchen, where Martha had been the sole keeper of the big bubbling pot for the past hour.

Will tugged Mina down the rest of the stairs and shepherded her over to his uncle. "Thank you, sir. This is no small honor—" Will's voice choked.

And she didn't blame him. What a marvel, how things had turned out.

Uncle Barlow clapped him on the back. "I think we can all thank Miss Whymsy. The whole idea was hers. Oh, except for this. . ." His face sobered. "I have arranged for your mother to be moved to the institute as soon as she is well enough to travel. I hope to make things right by her. No one should have to fear their own family."

The world turned watery, and Mina blinked back happy tears. *Thank You, God, for taking such a twisted situation and straightening it out.*

Will's throat bobbed several times before he answered. "You are more than gracious, sir. I can only hope to someday become the man that you are."

"I'd say you're well on your way, but remember these words, my boy. 'Whatever I have tried to do in life, I have tried with all my heart to do well; . . .whatever I have devoted myself to, I have devoted myself to completely; that in great aims and in small, I have always been thoroughly in earnest.'" Uncle turned his smile toward her. "Can you name that one?"

Joy swelled in her heart and spilled over into a large grin, for in the speaking of a single quote, she knew she'd been well and truly forgiven by Uncle Barlow. "From *David Copperfield*, sir." She hugged the book tucked beneath her arm all the tighter.

He chuckled. "Spot on. I shall have to work harder in the future to baffle you, hmm?"

"Oh, Mr. Barlow." Miss Whymsy crooked a finger at Will's uncle, beckoning him to her side. "If you wouldn't mind, a moment please?"

"Of course," he answered, then bent his head closer to Will and Mina, speaking for their ears alone. "Mum's the word for now, but don't be surprised if another wedding follows shortly after yours."

The old fellow turned on his heel and darted off before either of them could reply—and a good thing too for Mina was speechless. How amazing. How happy. How kind of God to have worked out such a perfect ending.

She peered up at Will, memorizing the joy on his face. Who knew what hardships the new year would bring, but for now, she'd live in this moment—in his gaze of love. "Oh, Will. How happy I am—"

"Congratulations, Cousin." Percy brushed past her and stopped in front of Will. "I guess you got what you wanted."

"No, not quite."

Will's words jolted through her. What more could he possibly want?

"There is one more thing that I desire." He held out the second-chance coin. "To give you this."

Percy snatched away the bit of gold in a trice. "What is it?"

"I am the man I am today because Uncle Barlow—and God— gave me a second chance. I'd like to do the same for you. I will speak to Uncle about seeing to your creditors, if you promise to stop your wild money-making schemes and get yourself an honest job. In fact,

I happen to know of a law clerk position that will be opening up shortly."

Her heart swelled. William Barlow was a hero after all. . .*her* hero.

Percy narrowed his eyes. "What's the catch?"

"There is none."

"Don't be ridiculous. Surely you expect something out of me for such a save." Percy cocked his head like a curious tot. "What is it?"

"I neither expect nor require anything. Don't you see? This is your chance to earn an honest living. Granted, it's not much, but there's opportunity for you to work your way up. Of course you don't deserve it, but neither did I when Uncle first offered me the position. And God knows none of us deserve His mercy—yet it is freely given. I cannot do otherwise. So, what do you say?"

Percy blinked. Then blinked some more. "Well. I. . .I don't quite know what to say."

Grabbing two mugs off a passing tray, Will handed one to his cousin and held up the other. "How about you say Happy Christmas and leave it at that?"

"What's this about?" Alice asked as she joined Percy's side.

For a moment, Percy frowned, then slowly reached with his free hand and pulled Alice close. "Happy Christmas, to our cousins." He clinked his mug against Will's and took a big draw.

With a laugh, Will swigged a drink, set the mug down, and gathered Mina into his arms.

She smiled up at him. "You really are a hero, you know."

"I wouldn't go that far." He kissed the top of her head. "But it seems this has turned out to be the best Christmas ever."

"It is, my love." She nuzzled her face against his shoulder. "That it is. And may we have many more."

Historical Notes

Christmas Pudding
Christmas pudding is quite a production, one that begins well before Christmas Day. In fact, it begins on Stir-Up Sunday, the last Sunday before Advent (or five weeks before Christmas). This is why when Mina returns home from dinner at Uncle Barlow's, she sees the pudding moulds on the kitchen table even though it's not yet Christmas.

Victorian Oyster Stew
Oysters have been savored in Britain since the days of the Romans. By Victorian times, industrialization cheapened oysters to the point of them becoming a staple of the poor man's diet, and they were a common fare served in public houses. This, however, depleted their abundance, and by the mid-1800s, the natural oyster beds became exhausted, making it harder to find good oysters. While other foods were served as well on Christmas Eve, oyster stew was as common as goose or turkey.

"God Rest Ye Merry, Gentlemen"
The origins of this song are controversial, with some claiming it dates back to the fifteenth century and others saying it didn't appear until 1760. Regardless, Victorians knew it well. Even Charles Dickens included it in *A Christmas Carol*.

Drinking Chocolate
What we now call cocoa or hot chocolate was called drinking chocolate in the mid-1800s. This beverage was a favorite among

Victorian ladies. You can find recipes for it even from the Regency period (early 1800s).

Florence Nightingale and the Institute for the Care of Sick Gentlewomen

Despite opposition from her family, Florence Nightingale became the Superintendent at the Institution for the Care of Sick Gentlewomen in Distressed Circumstances in London. Because of her, the facility began accepting patients of all religions, not just those allegiant to the Church of England. She received no salary and was responsible for her own expenses.

Secret Societies

Victorians were intrigued by the idea of covert meetings and secret societies. Many of these "clubs" dabbled in the supernatural, but a fair amount of them pursued social justice. While the norm was fraternal fellowships, there were also sororities or "sisterhoods."

ACKNOWLEDGMENTS

There are so many people who had a hand in bringing this story to you, but namely I'd like to thank the best critique buddies a girl could have: Yvonne Anderson, Julie Klassen, Elizabeth Ludwig, Shannon McNear, Ane Mulligan, Chawna Schroeder, and MaryLu Tyndall.

A hearty round of applause as well to Annie Tipton, the awesome editor who took a chance on me in the first place.

And last but definitely not least, much gratitude to my hero husband, Mark, who also happens to be my true BFF.

About the Author

Michelle Griep has been writing since she first discovered blank wall space and Crayolas. She seeks to glorify God in all that she writes—except for that graffiti phase she went through as a teenager. She resides in the frozen tundra of Minnesota, where she teaches history and writing classes for a local high school co-op. An Anglophile at heart, she runs off to England every chance she gets under the guise of research. Really though, she's eating excessive amounts of scones and rambling through some castle. Keep up with her adventures at michellegriep.com. She loves to hear from readers, so go ahead and rattle her cage.

Coming fall 2019

The journey continues in. . .

The Old Lace Shop

Book 3 in the Once Upon a Dickens Christmas series

A Novel by Michelle Griep

ENJOY THIS EXTENDED PREVIEW!

CHAPTER ONE

London, 1855

I have long abhorred black. It is a great abyss, sucking in the colours of the rainbow and wringing the life from them. The moniker of death. So it is no great loss when I slam the lid on the chest, shutting away my widow's weeds. Forever. I rise from my knees, and a genuine smile curves my lips.

"Mrs. White?" Betty raps at my chamber door and peeks her head inside. Her bleached apron is stark against her black servant's gown, and my smile fades. How much would it cost to reissue the staff with pewter-grey liveries instead? I determine to take it up with the solicitor when he arrives in an hour.

"Yes, Betty?" I soften my tone for she is a skittish little thing. Harsh words make her flinch even now, though it's been a year since my husband railed and raged about the townhouse.

"My pardon for disturbing you, mum." She dips her head. "But a Mr. Barlow is here, awaiting you in the sitting room."

"Barlow?" I roll the name around with my tongue, taste it, and find it a completely foreign flavor. "Who is that?"

The ruffle on Betty's cap trembles where it meets her brow. "Says he's with Smudge and Gruber, mum."

I glance at the clock ticking away on the mantel. Fifty-six minutes remain until I expect Mr. Smudge. Frowning, I thank Betty, and ponder who and why the mysterious Mr. Barlow is awaiting me.

A loose curl flops into my eye, and for a moment I consider leaving the rogue to bounce free, for that is what I am today. Finally and completely my own person...leastwise once Mr. Smudge arrives and I sign all the paperwork. But then a shadow clouds my mind, as dark and black as the mourning gowns I've laid to rest. Was this Mr. Barlow here with ill tidings about Mr. Smudge?

I pin the offending hair into place and leave my chamber. Memories bombard me like thrown tomatoes as I scurry down the corridor. There, where September sun shines through the windowpanes, the place where my husband threatened to push me out the glass. I shudder and speed past the vigil lantern on the hall table, the one that carved a small scar into my neck when he'd swung it at me. And at the top of the stairs, I take a moment to press my hand to my stomach. How many times had Mr. White tormented me by saying he ought to shove me down the stairway and be done with me?

Ghosts. All ghosts. I remind myself that my husband is well and truly gone and descend the stairs—hopefully for one of the last times. It will not be soon enough that I may leave behind this house of horror.

A thick man, hardly much taller than I, stands looking out through the sheers at Wellington Street, either enthralled by the day's traffic or lost in thought. Hard to tell. I clear my throat before I greet him. When he turns, sunlight bounces off his spectacles, and I blink.

"Good day, Mrs. White." He bows his head, and though I try to place the fellow with his dark hair and somewhat pasty skin, I cannot. "Mr. Percival Barlow, clerk to Mr. Gruber, at your service."

I take a seat on the settee and direct him to an adjacent chair. A small alarm begins to buzz at the back of my mind. Why was this fellow here instead of my lawyer? "To what do I owe this visit, Mr. Barlow?"

He settles a leather messenger bag on his lap and unbuckles the straps while he speaks. "Normally I make the rounds for Mr. Gruber. He is unlike Mr. Smudge in that he rarely leaves the office.

However, today I take it upon myself to add Mr. Smudge's clients to my stops as well." He pauses to pull out a sheaf of papers, then lifts his face to me. "I regret to inform you that your lawyer, Mr. Smudge, took a fall from a horse yesterday and broke his leg. In short, I am here to get your signature on the documents that he'd intended for you to sign."

He hands over the papers, and I page through them. Strange how a lifetime of ambition can be condensed into nothing more than a stack of parchment.

Mr. Barlow offers me a pen. "Each document represents one of your deceased husband's holdings. Sign your name on the bottom lines and the businesses will be sold, the proceeds of which shall come to you."

It is a bittersweet legacy. One that scratches as sharply as the nib with which I write my signature on the first page, selling off a dry goods warehouse in Birmingham. Surely Mr. White is rolling over in his grave. He'd married me, a girl five decades his junior, in order to avoid such a travesty of dying without an heir—and made me pay with each passing year that I didn't give him a son.

"You should be very well off for the rest of your days, Mrs. White." Mr. Barlow's voice pulls me from my thoughts. "I daresay you shall be able to do whatever it is you fancy."

The truth of his words slams into me, and my pen hovers above the line on the last page. Of course. He is right. But the only fancy I'd clung to the past year was the hope of leaving behind this townhouse and settling elsewhere, far from London. Escaping the past. Starting a whole new chapter of life. But what? And where? I'd been so preoccupied with flight that I'd not given a thought as to where I'd land.

My gaze sharpens on the heading of the page in my lap. *"Nottingham Lace and Hose."* Nottingham? Why not? That would be as good a place as any.

I set the pen on the tea table then hold out the unsigned paper to Mr. Barlow. "Tell me of this business, sir."

His big eyes widen as he grasps the page between finger and thumb, and while he silently reads, his lips fold into a pout. "It appears this is a lace manufacturing company, one of your husband's smaller holdings. His possession was at 51 percent, making him the majority owner but not by much. It says here"—he spears his finger midway down the document—"that the co-owner intends to purchase that share for sole proprietorship."

Mr. Barlow shoves the paper back at me. "Not to worry, Mrs. White. There is nothing untoward about this paper. Simply sign it, and I shall be on my way."

But I clench my hands in my lap, leaving the paper to dangle from Mr. Barlow's fingers. "Tell me, sir, what happens if I do not sign that document?"

"Not sign?" His head recoils as if I've slapped him. "Why would you not? Surely you do not intend to pursue the majority ownership of some small, dismal manufacturing company up in the middle of nowhere. For without your signature on that page, the holding falls to you. . .an unheard of position for a woman."

The small hairs at the back of my neck bristle. It may be a poor decision, but I've been told one too many times what to do, how to live, when to breathe and eat and walk. A scream wells in my throat, and I use the energy of it to lift my chin. "Yes, Mr. Barlow. That is exactly what I intend."

His wide mouth parts, then closes, as if words have bunched up behind his teeth and he's too afraid to let them loose. Finally, he sinks back against the cushion. "Are you certain of this, Mrs. White? It's a different world north of here, and manufacturing is a harsh and unforgiving trade. I fear a woman of your stature may not last long in such an environment."

I stifle a smile. He can have no idea that his opposition only serves to empower me. Though he may very well be correct, whatever may come of this, at least it will be because of my own choice.

"I am certain, sir."

His pasty skin greys to the shade of yesterday's porridge, and he fumbles inside his coat pocket to pull out a beat-up gold coin. He holds it out to me.

I've never seen the likes of it. The edges are chipped and gouged. A raised *X* takes up the most of one side. Words I can't read encircle the other. I angle my head at the man. "What is this?"

"It's a second-chance coin, Mrs. White." He pushes the paper for Nottingham Lace and Hose back at me across the tea table. "I should like to give you a second chance to reconsider your decision."

I lift my palm with the coin atop it. "No need, sir. My mind is quite made up."

He blows out a sigh, the kind that condemns me for being such a daft female, and rises to his feet, collecting all the papers save for the lace company. "Then I suppose I am finished here. I bid you good day, madam. And good luck."

I rise as well, following him with his coin. "But your coin, sir."

Pausing on the threshold, he turns to me. "Keep it. I have a feeling you may have need of it. I only wish I had a third and fourth chance coin to give you as well."

He pivots, and I am left alone with a piece of cold metal in my hand and a knotted bundle of hope and fear in my belly.

Am I doing the right thing?

Don't Miss the First in the Series!

12 Days at Bleakly Manor
Book 1

When Clara Chapman receives an intriguing invitation to spend Christmas at an English manor home, she is hesitant yet compelled to attend—for if she remains the duration of the twelve-day celebration, she is promised a sum of five hundred pounds. Imprisoned unjustly, Ben wants revenge on whoever stole his honor. Brought together under mysterious circumstances, Clara and Ben discover that what matters most is what Christmas is all about . . . love.

Paperback / 978-1-68322-258-3 / $12.99

Book 3—*The Old Lace Shop*—Coming September 2019!